DARK MUSIC
SHORT STORIES

Published by Compass Flower Press
an imprint of AKA-Publishing
Columbia. Missouri
www.AKA-Publishing.com

ISBN: 978-1-942168-53-9
Also available in eBook: ISBN: 978-1-942168-35-5

DARK MUSIC

SHORT STORIES

MIKE TRIAL

Acknowledgements

My thanks to the usual group: Yola, Frank, Tabitha, Geoff, Theresa. Your suggestions have helped me see deeper into the lives of the characters in these stories.

TABLE OF CONTENTS

String of Pearls

Grande Prairie Royal Canadian Airbase was the last stop on the aircraft ferry flights from the assembly plant in Indiana to the US Army Air Force base at Juneau, Alaska. It was built only to refuel planes en route to somewhere else. Eighteen months earlier it had been unbroken Alberta prairie, but with a ten-thousand-foot runway bulldozed level and covered with perforated steel plate, fuel facilities installed, one hangar built, and a half dozen Quonset huts and tents set up, it was an airbase. There was one road in and out—two hundred miles to Edmonton.

At 5 AM the base PA system screeched to life and began blaring something that might have been "Reveille." Ann pried herself out of her warm bunk, dressed in the oversized men's flight suit all the women pilots wore, pulled a comb through her hair, and stumbled out into the Canadian darkness to stand early morning formation with the rest of the airfield troops.

Fog haloed the two streetlights that lit the area between the barracks where formations were held. Orders of the day were read, which had nothing to do with the women pilots. An officious corporal in the Royal Canadian Flying Corps came to the end of the row where the three American women stood. He studied his clipboard in the dim light, then called roll:

"Alban, Ann."

"Here," Ann said quietly, wondering what he would do if she wasn't there.

"Benson, Sally."

"Here, and ready for action, sir!" Sally answered heartily. The corporal glared at her.

"Murdock, Iris."

"Here."

The corporal disappeared, and the formation was dismissed. The three women slogged through the half-frozen mud to the mess hall.

"Why do we have to stand formation with the base staff?" Sally asked Iris, as she did every morning. Iris was the leader of the flight simply by being assigned that role back at the Republic Aircraft manufacturing plant in Indiana. From some hidebound town in Vermont, she was a natural leader—tall, slim, decisive, her dark hair cropped very short. Sally more closely resembled Dinah Shore, whom she admired, with her blond hair, ready smile, and cheerful disposition. But she was not a scatterbrained blond. Sally had gotten very high scores for aircraft handling in flight school and could land even the notorious P-47 as smoothly as any man in the US Army Air Corps.

"Military courtesy, Sally. Military courtesy," Iris told her patiently. Iris adhered to military custom even though the WASP—the Women Airforce Service Pilots organization—was a civil service organization, not part of the military. Inside the steamy mess tent they got hot coffee and whatever slop was being served for breakfast, and dug in.

"This fog's going to be a problem," Sally ventured.

Ann shook her head. "Not really. We can climb above this stuff here; it will dissipate as the sun warms the land. It's the fog rising up the west side of the mountains from the ocean that's going to be the problem."

Iris nodded emphatically. "That's right. Once we pass the crest of the mountains we'll be descending into fog, dew point and temp are going to be within a couple of degrees of each other, which means low visibility and icing conditions. We can't stay high, up in colder air, or we'll miss the Juneau beacon."

Sally's face was somber. "Ice on the plane, loss of lift, control surfaces unresponsive. I don't like it. And we'll be low on fuel."

"Nobody does. But we'll make it. But the fuel situation means that we can't turn back once we're over the mountains." Iris's thin lips tightened. "We've got to get our navigation right. Straight line to the beacon on the east face of the mountains, then turn to heading 300, get over the crest, and a straight-line descent to Juneau field. If all goes well, we'll only be in the fog for twenty minutes."

Ann visualized the last twenty minutes of the six-hour flight facing them. They'd be fighting exhaustion while coping with mountaintops obscured by fog, along with potential icing and low fuel. She rolled her head to ease the tension that was already building in her neck.

Iris pulled her leather helmet back on. "I'm going to the weather shack. They're going to release weather balloons in a few minutes. I want to see if they revise the weather forecast. You two preflight the planes."

The three thick-bodied P-47 fighter aircraft squatted on the parking apron like Cretaceous reptiles, noses tilted at the hazy sky. And that's what they were, Ann thought, 2,600-horsepower killing machines, meant to fly fast and annihilate enemy planes and ground targets with a hundred rounds per second of .50-caliber machine gun fire.

Ann ignored the cold and concentrated on methodically checking everything on the preflight checklist. A full thirty minutes later, she was finished and confident the aircraft was in proper working order. Ann and Sally then each did one side of Iris's plane.

"These aircraft look fine to me," Sally said cheerfully. Even at 7:30 in the morning, dressed in a bulky flight suit, with a leather flying helmet over her blond hair, she managed to look attractive. Ann, who had always considered herself too plain and too studious, had envied Sally from the day they met in primary flight training in Columbia, Missouri. But despite her good looks, Sally was not in the least pretentious. She and Ann had become best friends.

"These planes should be in top shape," Ann said. "They're brand new." She paused. "To tell you the truth, Sally," Ann continued slowly, "I'm still a little tense flying these P-47s."

"You shouldn't be—you had the best overall scores in the P-47 of our whole class." Sally looked at the huge twelve-foot-diameter prop on the nearest plane. "Didn't that old guy back at Avenger field, the classroom instructor, Lieutenant Cochrane, tell us, 'A little tension will make you a better pilot'?"

"A little tension, maybe. But I feel a lot of tension." Ann took a deep breath. "Lieutenant Cochrane wasn't old. Thirty-five maybe."

"So what? I'm twenty-three, so he's an old guy."

Thirty minutes later Ann and Sally were still standing in the fog waiting for Iris.

"What's taking her so long?" Ann said. Her teeth were starting to chatter.

Sally laughed her silvery laugh. "Iris probably decided to get it on with that chubby tech sergeant in the weather shack."

The image of those two making love was so ridiculous that a bark of laughter slipped out of Ann. "Sorry. I'm tense."

Sally's smile faded. "Me too. I don't like the idea of descending into icing conditions with mountaintops right below us. I don't like it one little bit. These planes are hard enough to fly in good weather."

"Maybe Iris is getting approval to delay the flight until there's better weather."

Sally shrugged. "Not likely. You heard what she said. The Russians want these planes immediately. They don't care what the flying conditions are. I heard the Russian army has had a million casualties already. Stalin doesn't care how many of his own people die, or Americans, as long as the Germans don't take his empire away from him."

"They're just trying to defend Russia..."

"Whatever they think they're doing, they need some lessons in what Iris calls 'military courtesy.' A bunch of them were down at Avenger field the week we graduated. Remember? I never saw such a bunch of juvenile jerks, with their off-color jokes and constant leering at us. Worse than my high school boyfriend." Sally's voice faded away in the cold fog. "Not like those guys we met back in Columbia." Sally laughed and clapped her hands. "Remember that night we double-dated? Went to that place near campus?"

Ann smiled. "Yeah, I wish I was back there right now."

Iris's tall form emerged from the fog, her long-faced New England features creased in tension. "This fog is going to be here for three more days, at least.

Worse on the other side of the mountain. We're at high risk for icing." Iris shook her head and looked like she was considering spitting. "And this fine... airbase," she continued, "only has enough avgas to fill our tanks three quarters full. They say the fuel truck's due today, but they said that yesterday too." Iris pulled a creased paper from her baggy flight suit. "WASP Headquarters is screaming that the Russians need these aircraft immediately." She stuffed the paper back in her pocket. "No choice. We've got to fly today."

"So..." Ann said slowly, "they insist we fly over the mountains into icing conditions, and find the Juneau airstrip in the fog, with no fuel to spare if our navigation is off."

"I think we should wait a day," Sally said. "Fog might start to clear tomorrow."

"We'll fly today; this morning. It's December, so it starts getting dark in Juneau by sixteen hundred hours," Iris said. "I don't want to add a night landing at Juneau to our troubles." She paused, sliding back her flight-suit sleeve to see the big silver watch she wore. "It's 08:30. We'll wait until 09:30 to let the fog on this side of the mountains dissipate a little, and to see if a fuel truck shows up. Then we push off. Wheels up at ten hundred hours." Iris squinted at the hazy sky. "You girls go back to the Quonset; I'm going to wait in the weather shack." Sally gave Ann a wink that Iris didn't notice. "I'll come and get you at 09:30."

Lying on their bunks in the ten-by-ten plywood cubicle in the Quonset was torture. Even the usually ebullient Sally just lay staring at the ceiling. Some nights on these stopovers, Sally would dance the foxtrot around the oil stove with an imaginary partner while she hummed "A String of Pearls." Sally loved that song, and so did Ann.

Ann thought of her mother and father back on the farm in Missouri. Sometimes her mother would put their one Glenn Miller record on the Victrola, and she and Ann's father would dance around the living room. Ann felt tears beginning to well up, blanked those memories out of her mind, and went back to concentrating on the bare plywood ceiling. Her heart pounded steadily in her chest. Outside in the fog, the big unforgiving P-47 waited for her. And six hundred miles west loomed the sawtooth peaks of the Rockies.

Eventually it was time. The weather had not changed, and the fuel truck had not appeared.

"Don't forget," Iris said as she tapped the blue-gray wing of her aircraft, "we are taking off with fuel tanks only three quarters full. Stay at cruise speed to conserve fuel. We fly a straight-line course to the beacon on the eastern slope of the mountains. Fly directly over it so we'll see the signal drop then come back on. When it does, immediately take up heading 300 magnetic for Juneau, and climb to 12,000. We should be over the crest in thirty minutes, and we should then be able to pick up the Juneau signal." Iris extended her arm to the northwest. "Heading 340 straight to the beacon on this side of the mountains." She pivoted and extended her arm to the southwest. "Climb to 12,000 on heading 300. After thirty minutes, begin a slow descent straight holding heading 300 straight in to Juneau. Everything check out on the aircraft?" Ann and Sally nodded. "Then let's go take one last pee, and be on our way," Iris said.

Three hours later, with the three aircraft at 8,000 feet descending in fog, Ann hoped they were past the last of the mountain crests. She reviewed in her mind what Lieutenant Cochrane had taught them about flying the P-47 in icing conditions: "If you are getting ice buildup on the airfoil surfaces, you'll start losing airspeed, and the controls will feel very heavy. Enough ice, and even full throttle won't keep you in the air. If you see ice on the wings, or the controls feel heavy and your airspeed is dropping for no apparent reason, you've got ice, and you need to get out of the icing conditions immediately."

Ann could see no sign of ice on the blue-gray wing surfaces. But in-flight ice was clear and could accumulate almost imperceptibly. She waggled the stick. Controls still felt light. No icing on the control surfaces. With the mountains below them, and only enough fuel to make Juneau on a straight-in approach, they had no choice but to press ahead.

Ann realized she was leaning forward against the shoulder straps again, and she sat back against her parachute, trying to relax a little. Maybe it was her imagination, but her airspeed seemed to have dropped a bit. Ann pushed in a touch more power, and airspeed increased to 360.

"I think I'm getting some ice," Sally said on the inter-aircraft radio, her voice tight. "Controls feel heavy. I'm at 3,000 RPM, but airspeed has dropped to 340."

"Go to full power," Iris ordered. "Close cowl flaps to half open. Engine heat should help de-ice."

Sally was silent, then, "Still losing airspeed."

"Increase rate of descent to 500 feet per minute!" Iris ordered. "But keep your wings level and do not reduce power!"

Ann knew a mountain crag could appear out of the haze in an instant, but they had no choice.

There was a gasp on the radio, a grunt, then Sally's voice: "Dammit, straighten up, you bitch!"

Silence.

"Benson, respond!" Iris said.

Silence.

"Alban, respond!"

"Here," Ann said.

"Do you have any visual contact—mountains, Benson's aircraft, anything?"

Ann squinted hard into the haze. "Negative; nothing. I'm at 8,000 feet..."

"Benson, respond," Iris repeated.

There was only silence on the radio.

"Benson, respond!" Iris repeated again.

"I'm turning back to look for her," Ann said.

"Negative!" Iris shouted into the radio. "Turn back, and you won't have enough fuel to make Juneau. If she's down, we can't help her."

Ann twisted her radio frequency dial over to UNICOM. "Canadian forces! Canadian forces!" she shrieked. "American aircraft down at coordinates 136 West 57 North. Send air rescue..." Her voice choked on a sob, and she released the radio transmit button. She turned the dial back to inter-aircraft.

"...centrate on your flying, Alban!" Iris's voice was taut. "Hold heading 300, keep your RPM up, and hold airspeed at 360."

"If we turn back, we might be able to spot her," Ann sobbed. "If Sally is down there..."

"Negative!" Iris snapped. "We'll run out of fuel searching for her. You concentrate on flying your aircraft! Nothing else!"

Ann pulled up her goggles to let tears flow, but kept her wings level, steady descent rate, airspeed at 360. The endless minutes went by. Several times she thought she saw indistinct gray crags in the haze below.

Then the Juneau signal began to flicker on the radio direction finder, and the haze began to thin. More minutes passed, and in the distance Ann saw the straight gray line that was Juneau's 10,000-foot airstrip.

Both her fuel gauge needles were tapping their empty pins when Ann flared her aircraft into a letter-perfect landing at Juneau Army Airfield. She taxied to where the ground crew stood, pivoted the plane, and went through the engine shutdown checklist. The engine coughed to a halt.

After a while, she realized someone was tapping on the canopy. A fresh-faced boy in cold-weather coveralls with tech sergeant stripes was peering in. "You alright, ma'am?"

Ann nodded, unstrapped herself, and unlatched the canopy. The kid helped her flip it over to the side. She could barely clamber out into the cold wind.

"Rough flight?"

"The worst."

Ann climbed down from the big airplane and stood on the PSP mat, staring at the dark mountains they'd just crossed. Iris came over and stood silently beside her. "There's nothing either of us could have done, Ann. Sally's plane went down. She's gone."

And then Iris did something Ann had never seen in the eight months she had known her. She turned away from Ann, covered her face with her hands, and stood shaking with muffled sobs. Ann felt her own tears start, and she rubbed them away with her hands.

After a moment, Iris got herself back under control and turned to face the five Russians in brown uniforms who were approaching in the gathering dark.

The two women and the five Russians stood looking at each other for a moment, then one Russian stepped forward. His shoulder boards were no help guessing his rank. "Another plane, where?" He pantomimed looking around the horizon. "Tomorrow come?"

"No," Iris explained. She held up one finger. "One plane," she said, pantomiming a plane spiraling down, "boom, kaput."

The Russians spoke among themselves for a time.

"Three plane," the man said. "We need. How soon another?"

Iris shook her head. "I'll have to contact..."

"After, after, tomorrow?" The man stepped forward, chin jutting.

Iris shrugged. "I don't know." She and Ann turned toward the ready room.

The Russian caught Iris's shoulder and turned her around. His expression was hard. "Three plane...we need, very bad!" He made a cutting motion with one hand. "We need. Wehrmacht coming, coming..."

Ann felt a steel cable inside her break. She hurled herself onto the angry Russian, pummeling him with fists, tearing at his tunic. He staggered back while his men gaped. Ann screamed in his face, "You stupid Russians! Bastards! Goddam Russians! Sally wouldn't be dead if it weren't for you...you bastards!" She clawed at the Russian, who tried to protect himself with hands and arms. His heel caught in the perforated steel plate of the mat, and he went over backward, Ann on top of him pounding him in a whirlwind of fists.

She felt hands pull her off. And then Iris was walking her away, and suddenly all energy drained out of her. She was aware of the Russian being helped to his feet, shouting at her. He slapped his pistol, pushed his men away, and stomped away toward the Russian barracks on the other side of the field.

Iris helped Ann into the transient barracks Quonset and into one of the plywood cubicles. She unrolled the mattress on a lower bunk, spread an army blanket, laid Ann down, untied her bootlaces, and got her to stretch out. She covered her with two blankets and made sure the stove was burning on low. "I've got to file my report. Don't you leave this room, understand?"

Ann woke in the darkness of the cubicle. Night had come. Iris lay under her blankets on the other lower bunk. The oil stove softly hissed, its dim glow lighting the cubicle. *I wish I could be like Iris*, Ann thought, *put the tragedy out of my mind, focus on the moment only. But I can't.* Ann remembered Sally putting her hair up like Dinah Shore and dancing around the oil stove humming "A String of Pearls." The sobs inside her rose up again. She held the blanket to her mouth to keep from waking Iris.

The next day dawned foggy and cold. Ann, in a state of shock, sat through four hours of reports and questioning by a captain from the Flight Safety Office. She filled out the forms the best she could, answered questions the best she could, and tried not to think.

Eventually it ended. Iris had gotten them space-available seats on a battered C-47 that would carry them to Hamilton Army Airfield, California—the first leg of their journey back to WASP headquarters.

With an overnight stop, the trip to California took two days.

In the cold gloom of the aircraft, Ann huddled in her flight jacket and an army blanket as the endless hours passed. She and Iris sat like zombies most of the time, trying to sleep in the noisy gloom of the windowless airplane, occasionally getting up to stretch their legs. Once Ann was horrified to see Iris's face contorted with anguish, tears running down her cheeks as she sat silent and rigidly erect. Ann pretended not to see.

They climbed out of the C-47 into the surreal warmth and sunshine of Northern California. Shedding their flight jackets, they lugged their gear to the in-processing office, where they joined the end of a line of men waiting for standby flight assignments. Once they'd worked their way to the front of the line, they were told, "You won't get a flight today," by a harried E4. He handed them a slip of paper. "But we've got space in temporary quarters. Women's barracks, building 122-W-22. Chow hall's two blocks toward the flight line from there. Check back here at 0800 tomorrow." He scribbled on a piece of paper, handed it to Iris, and turned his attention to the next person in line.

"Why don't you stay here with all our gear while I go find this place," Iris said.

Ann sat on their flight bags, leaning against the adobe wall of one of the old buildings from when this was a cavalry base. The mild California sun felt good on her face.

After a while, Iris returned, and they made their way to a third-floor open-bay bunk room in a refurnished adobe building. The sign over the door said WOMEN'S QUARTERS! KEEP OUT! Iris and Ann selected a top and bottom bunk that didn't have people's things on them.

"You hungry?" Iris said, looking at her watch. "The chow line may still be running."

"Not really," Ann said. "I just want to get back to Indiana and get our next assignment."

Iris nodded. "Yeah, I guess I do too. Let's walk over to Ops and see what the chances are for a flight tomorrow."

Down the hill in the Operations Center, half a dozen enlisted men were filling out manifests, scheduling flights and crews, scurrying back and forth to the clipboards on the wall that listed current flights and manifests. The activity was good for Ann's nerves. The sunshine and silence of the beautifully preserved adobe barracks up on the hill had been a bit too fast a return to peace and beauty for her mind to accept. It was good to hear the radio, aircraft out on the runway, the tower radio responding.

There were nearly thirty clipboards on the wall, each with a flight number, destination, departure time, and a handwritten list of cargo and passengers.

"Here's a flight to Arlington Field via Tucson," Iris said. "Looks like they've still got some space." She took the clipboard over to the desk.

"Be with you ladies in a minute," a flustered E6 told them. Iris laid the clipboard on the desk. The minutes went by, and the activity of the men behind the desk didn't diminish.

Iris eventually caught the attention of an overweight E4 back of the desk whose expression said, *I'm too busy for this.* "We'd like to put our names on this flight, standby to Arlington Field, Texas," she told him.

He picked up the clipboard, checked a list on the table behind him, then shuffled through a wire basket full of documents, found what he wanted, and came around the end of the desk to confront the two women.

Out from behind the elevated desk, he was at least two inches shorter than Iris.

"Well, ma'am," he said, his voice dripping sarcastic Southern courtesy, "I don't think I can get y'all on that flight."

"Perhaps there's another flight..." Iris began reasonably.

"Not for you," the kid drawled. He held a document up. "Y'all are members of the WASPs, right?"

Ann and Iris nodded.

His smiled widened. "Well, that organization has been disbanded as of 20 October. You ain't eligible to fly on military aircraft no more." Iris snatched the paper out of his hand and scanned it, handed it to Ann. It was true. The WASPs had been disbanded.

Ann was shocked beyond words; she simply stood there staring. Iris took the paper back and stared at it while the smarmy E4 yammered on.

"...and of course, we're always happy to extend military courtesy rides to our girls in uniform, but since y'all ain't part of the military no more, that courtesy don't apply."

Iris looked up from the paper with a glare that would have scorched paint. "Courtesy doesn't apply?" Like lightning, she pulled back a fist and planted a gut punch in fatso's belly with every one of her rangy 140 pounds behind it. Fatso doubled over and staggered back into one of the wooden chairs along the wall.

The men behind the desk looked at him, then at Iris. A couple of them grinned. Nobody went to help chubby up.

Iris tossed the paper on the counter, caught Ann's elbow, and marched her smartly out into the sunshine. Ann had to suppress a hysterical laugh as she trotted to keep up.

Back at the barracks, Ann's energy dissipated. She sat on her bunk. "The WASPs disbanded! I can't believe it. Now what?"

Iris put her flight bag on her bunk and started pulling everything out of it. Outside the window, the sparrows chirping in the eaves seemed entirely unreal to Ann. The sounds from the airfield seemed very far away.

"Damned man-dominated War Department!" Iris spat. She paced. "General Spaatz will not pay the congressional price to get the WASP group named part of the Army Air Force. Well, aviation is here to stay, military or civilian, and I am going to be part of it."

Ann straightened up. "Doing what? They won't let you fly planes."

"I'll figure something out," Iris said grimly. "No matter what happens, I'm staying in aviation. No sense hanging around here. You and I are going to get in line at the train station with all the other civilians," Iris said briskly. "How's your money supply?"

Ann dug through her things. "Thirty-five dollars."

Iris held out a wad of bills. "I've got fifty-five. We'll divvy it up fifty-fifty, so here's ten dollars. That should be enough for each of us."

"To go where?" Ann said as she accepted the ten-dollar bill.

"I'm going to Washington," Iris told her. "My friend in G2 can get me a civilian position in aviation." She smiled and gave Ann a hug. "You go home, kid. Visit your parents. Then figure out what the next steps are, okay?"

Ann nodded, feeling like Raggedy Ann the rag doll, completely limp, completely passive.

Iris unfolded her flight bag and quickly transferred a few items into the canvas carry-bag the women took on board the planes they were flying—it was not much larger than a large purse. She left her other uniform and her fleece-lined leather flight jacket and leather helmet on the bunk. "Somebody else can have that stuff."

In the crowd at the train station, Iris and Ann awkwardly hugged. They had exchanged mailing addresses and promised to stay in touch, but as Iris's tall form faded into the crowd, Ann knew she would never see her again.

At the train station in Kansas City, her mother and father were waiting for her. During the ride home in their old Dodge, Ann in the back seat just like always, her mother chattered away about the dinner she was preparing to welcome her home. Her father said nothing, gripping the wheel with his work-warped hands. Ann could think of nothing to say.

At the house, Ann was exhausted but so nervous she couldn't sit still. She paced the small living room while her father stoked the woodstove.

"We're real proud of you, girl, your mother and me," he said, keeping his attention firmly on the flames beginning to take off in the split oak. "We've talked. We want you to stay with us, but we know you probably won't. Seen too much of the big world to want to live here on this 147 acres. We understand. You've already done more than most people in this county will ever do. But we'll..." His voice broke and for a moment he prodded the wood in silence. "... but we'll always be glad to see you come home for visits."

Ann, tears leaking from her eyes, fled up the stairs to her old room. The cold air of the room felt good—it matched the ice in her heart. She touched the wallpaper, the old wood dresser. "It's only been two years since I left this room," she whispered. "But I'm not me anymore." She sat on her bed staring out the window at the familiar contour of the harvested cornfield and beyond it the trees at the little creek she'd spent many hours exploring as a little girl. A tear fell onto her left hand.

I wish I had been the one who crashed in the mountains, not Sally. I can't come back to this.

After a moment she dried her tears, opened her flight bag, and took out her worn khaki shirt with its silver WASP wings. In the twilight, the wings on either side of the silver diamond looked real; the room around her did not. She hung the shirt in the closet. There was the rustle of paper. Ann dug out the crumpled note with Iris's mailing address and stared at it without seeing it. *WASP days may be over, but Iris is not leaving aviation, and I won't either. TWA in Kansas City may have openings for people with flight skills, even if it's just radio operator, or air traffic controller, or...anything.*

Ann smoothed the note out and laid it on the dresser, and for the first time since she'd walked into the house, she felt like she really was home.

In the top drawer of the dresser she found one of her old blouses and put it on. At the back of the drawer was a flat rectangular case labeled BEIDERMAN'S JEWELERS. She opened it with a smile and took out the strand of pearls her mother had given her when she graduated from high school. The pearls were cool and smooth and ghostly in the fading light—perfect spheres on a barely visible cord, a tiny knot on either side of each pearl. The women she had flown with, the WASPs, were a bit like this string of pearls—beautiful alone, but better in a strand put together so that even if one fell, not all of them would fall.

She thought for a moment of Sally, humming "A String of Pearls" and dancing around the oil stove with her imaginary dream lover. Then Ann wiped her tears away, put a smile on her face, and went downstairs to help her mother prepare supper.

CAT ISLAND

May 1978, Apostle Islands, Lake Superior, Wisconsin

A faraway cry woke Rick, who had been half asleep in one of the old lawn chairs in front of the campfire. The wood fire crackled softly. Another cry came, closer.

"Damned cats," Rick mumbled. He downed a slug of Jack Daniels from the bottle, found a flashlight, and advanced into the forest. He had not gone far when he saw movement. Cats! Two—no—three of them, digging and tearing at something on the ground. The feral cats that roamed the island could be dangerous. They weren't big, but they could be aggressive, and a bite or scratch would almost certainly become infected. He stepped one more step. The cats froze, staring at him, their eyes topaz in the yellow light, then they bounded silently into the darkness.

The flashlight's beam picked out white flecks where the cats had been working something out of the ground. He toed it with his boot. Bones. Big enough to be human vertebra. *Ojibwe burial*, Rick told himself, but there was also rotting cloth amongst the bones, a rag that looked like the collar of a plaid shirt. Not something an Indian would be buried in.

Rick reached down for it, but he could not seem to grasp it.

He started awake in the lawn chair, still reaching for something he couldn't quite grasp. *I'm drunk, dreaming; that's all it is.* He grabbed the Jack Daniels bottle at his feet and finished off what was left. *Those old Pendleton shirts me, and Tom, and Dave all wore back in '70s when we were working for Bill Payson Construction.* "But I doubt if anyone's ever been buried out here in a Pendleton shirt," he slurred. "Just a dream." He stumbled into the cabin and pulled his sleeping bag up around him.

Earlier, it had felt good sailing Dave's little sloop *Lucy* out to Cat Island. *Just like the old days.* The blue-grey water of Lake Superior, the sound of wind in the rigging, the slap of the waves, and the familiar island landmarks sliding by in the gathering dusk—it all felt good.

As he approached Cat Island's only cove, he came about sharply, lined up on the narrow entrance, and reefed the mainsail. *Lucy* glided into the narrow defile. As Rick tilted the outboard into the water and motored to the mooring, he breathed deep of the pine-scented air. *God, it's good to be back.*

Cat Island, only a hundred yards wide and a quarter of a mile long. Uninhabited, except for the feral cats that gave it its name. It was the least accessible of the islands on Lake Superior; it's cliff-like sides discouraged sailors wanting to put ashore. A perfect refuge.

A sunset the color of clotted blood had spread itself across the western sky by the time he had made his way to the clearing. The cabin was just as he remembered it. Back in the summer of 1971, he and Tom and Dave had built this cabin. Tom and Dave quickly lost interest in it, but Rick loved it. Almost every weekend until winter came, he'd sail out by himself, sit by the fire, watch the stars, listen to the wind in the pines, and try to turn his awkward guitar playing into music.

But now, in the gloomy twilight, he felt no sense of homecoming. The cabin seemed to glower at him. Inside, Rick slung his gear down on the sofa and got an oil lamp burning. The air was cold and tinctured with the scent of rotting meat. He searched the place, but there was nothing amiss. No dead mice, no rotting garbage, nothing. But the stench of putrescence hung in the still, dank air.

Damned feral cats, Rick thought. *They probably killed a raccoon and left the carcass in the crawlspace under the cabin. I'll clear it out tomorrow.*

Rick dug a fresh bottle of Jack Daniels out of his backpack and got a fire started in the fire pit. Once it was going, he hunched close, stolidly taking pulls at the bottle. The wind had died, but the night air was cold.

Yesterday Rick had been sitting behind the register at Hot Coffee in Duluth. It had been a mild spring evening, seven thirty and the sky was still a smear of orange behind the cranes at the port. Nobody was in the place but him and Tricia, just killing time until they could close. Rick had been leafing through the *Duluth Register* while Tricia unloaded the dishwasher in the back room. The place was always empty after six. Why Aaron kept it open until eight o'clock Rick couldn't understand. Who'd want coffee at eight o'clock at night?

Rick looked at the newspaper without interest, slowly turning the pages over, killing time. The summer rental ads were beginning to appear. "Rent your summer paradise in the Apostle Islands." Rick grinned. He recognized one of the "homes for rent" pictures. Payson Construction had built it. He stared at the houses backed by pine trees, the ads for boat trips, fishing excursions, and bicycles for rent.

He got his flask of bourbon out, found it empty, and slipped it back in his jacket pocket.

"Let's close up now," he called to Tricia. "The boss will never know."

She ignored him. He said that every night.

Rick got up and began pacing around the empty coffee shop as the need for another drink started to grow inside him. There was a fresh bottle of Jack Daniels waiting for him back at his apartment. And that was all that was waiting for him.

He stood at the window looking out at empty Sixth Street. *I've been renting that ratty little furnished apartment for a year and never had single guest: no girls, no friends, nobody.*

Just two bottles a day of oblivion and this part time job at Hot Coffee.

Rick looked at his reflection in the coffee shop door and the empty street beyond. He shook his head and whispered, "This is no life. I'm only twenty-six. I need . . ."

"What?" Tricia asked. "You finished sweeping up?"

"Yeah."

"I'm out of here." She grabbed her coat and purse and brushed past him. "Don't forget to set the auto lock on the door."

Rick stood for a moment, then went back to the newspaper. "I could rent a place back in La Pointe, get a job there, quit drinking so much . . ."

But he knew the few jobs on the island would already be taken. And he had no money saved up. He needed a job, even a no-brain job like this one.

He stared at an ad for half-day boat trips. "All the Apostle's beautiful, uninhabited islands. Perfect for hikes, picnics . . ." There was a little map. Rick found Cat Island.

"That's where I need to be. The little cabin on Cat Island. There's nothing for me in this town."

He wrote his resignation on a piece of paper and left it by the register.

A scratching sound woke him.

Rick got out of his sleeping bag, grabbed the flashlight, and went to the window. Fog was forming along the ground, but above the tops of the pines Aldebaran burned bright in the Hyades. He zipped up his jacket and went through the fog to where he dreamed he'd seen cats digging at bones.

There were no cats, no bones, no Indian grave, and no fragments of a plaid shirt, only some whitened pine sticks. He stood in starlit silence staring at the ground where he thought he'd seen cats tearing at a carcass and a scrap of an old shirt.. . . *Just a dream.*

He returned to the cabin and crawled back into his sleeping bag.

In 1970 they had all been eighteen, he and Dave and Tom. All finished with high school in Bayfield, all living in La Pointe for the summer, all working for

Bill Payson's construction company putting up the first summer homes on Madelaine Island.

It was the best of times: no responsibilities, good friends, hard work in the sunshine, drinking beer on the veranda in front of Elsie's store in the evening. They would chase after the summer girls who'd ride the ferry across from Bayfield. Except Dave, who had a steady girlfriend, Angela, a nurse at Ashland Hospital. Dave was already talking about getting married. Tom and Rick kidded him a good deal about that—and about Dave wanting to be shift foreman for Bill Payson.

"So you want to be our boss?" Tom grinned at Dave. "Rick and me, we may go ahead and take our union exams and organize a carpenters union here . . ."

"Besides," Rick told Dave, "Bill Payson's not going to pay you anything extra for being foreman. So why do you want the headache of updating schedules, filling out OSHA reports, holding the safety meetings, filling out workers comp forms, signing time sheets, checking material orders . . ."

Dave laughed. "Ambition, Rick, something you ought have a little more of. I'm going to own this company some day. Maybe someday you two will want to settle down and get married. Be something more than non-union, weekly-rate carpenters."

"I have ambition," Rick came back at him, stung a little bit.

Tom laughed. "Yeah, he wants to be a singer. You

ought to hear him singing while we're working: 'Band of Gold' or 'Fire and Rain.' Who's that by?"

"James Taylor," Rick said.

"You need to learn to play that old guitar of yours better," Tom told Rick, "if you're going to get the girls. I can teach you."

Rick nodded. Having Tom teach him would be good, but he didn't want Tom to know how impressed he was with Tom's easy way with his guitar. That was why Rick had bought his own guitar last month at the pawn shop in Bayfield and started chording along on the bits and pieces of top forty songs Tom would play. Most summer evenings they'd sit on the veranda in front of Elsie's store, drinking New Glaurus beer and playing. Rick could see the lustful looks Tom got from the girls walking by on their way back to the ferry. And Rick knew he wanted them to look at him that way too.

"Yeah," Rick said. "That would be great. I also want to write some of my own songs." Rick hadn't known until he said it, but the more he thought about it, the more he realized it was what he wanted. He wasn't going to study for his Carpenter's Union exam. And he wasn't going to keep working for Payson Construction for the rest of his life. He was going to be a musician. A real one, not some street singer playing for the tourists and not some bar guitarist playing "Close to You" for maudlin sailors off the ore ships in Duluth.

Rick learned fast. Pretty soon Rick and Tom had a repertoire of top forty tunes they'd play Wednesday evenings. By the time it was dark, there'd sometimes be ten or fifteen dollars in the guitar case they kept open. Rick and Tom would meticulously split the money 50-50. All of it went toward paying for the beer they were drinking.

Tom liked "Which Way You Goin', Billy?" and could make it sound pretty good. But Rick liked "Love Grows Where My Rosemary Goes," with its upbeat danceable melody. He knew he would have to play commercial stuff while he was getting his start, but he also knew he could write music better than what he heard on the radio. Already he was working out chord progressions for songs of his own.

Once in a while they'd get Dave to join them on an old keyboard he'd bought. Now people were stopping to listen, even making requests for certain songs, and once a guy and his girlfriend tossed a five-dollar bill in after they'd done a great job on the Edison Lighthouse song, "Love Grows."

"You're doing good, Rick," Tom encouraged. "No need to push so hard; this is supposed to be fun."

Then one Wednesday afternoon in May everything changed. A VW van drove off the ferry, up Second

Street, and stopped in front of Elsie's store where Rick and Tom had their usual table staked out. A girl with long brown hair stuck her face out the window and said, "Any of these empty stores for rent?" She was good-looking, but not gorgeous, but a great smile and a sultry voice.

Rick strolled over to the VW. "What's your name?"

She smiled up at him, and Rick thought she had the most beautiful eyes he'd ever seen. Blue grey, the same color as Lake Superior on a sunny day.

"Katie. What's yours?"

"I'm Rick," he said and tilted his head at the veranda. "That's Tom. Join us for a beer."

"Why not?" She parked her van, and took a chair at their table and accepted a cold bottle of New Glaurus beer.

Tom pointed to a closed shop two doors down. "That store's empty. Might be a good place. Lots of tourists walk past it coming up First Street from the ferry."

"Yeah," Rick added. "Clean it out, paint it, wash the windows, it would look real nice. "

"We'll help," Tom said. "And I know Andy Walker would give you a three month lease real cheap. He just wants somebody in the place to keep it from being vandalized."

"Three months is all I'd need," Katie said. "I'm moving to Seattle, but I'm out of money. Got to sell some of my paintings, then get on the road again before winter comes."

"I'll talk to Andy tomorrow," Tom said.

They worked every evening to get her art gallery, Gallery Evermore, open for business by Memorial Day weekend. They weren't expecting much, but people crowded in by the dozens. When Rick went out to get more beer, he brought his guitar back from the apartment and he and Tom played a few tunes. When Katie complimented them and started singing along with some of the tunes, it lit a fire inside Rick that he hadn't felt in a while.

Next Wednesday, Rick and Tom were tuning their guitars on the porch at Elsie's.

"Wish Dave was still playing with us. We need his keyboard backfill," Tom said, fingering his old Gibson.

Rick shook his head. "He can't spare the time any more. Got to drive down to Ashland right after work. Angela's kid is home alone after school."

"The married life." Tom grinned. "Elsie still storing his keyboard?"

Rick tuned his guitar. "I'm supposed to be looking for a buyer for it."

A couple of bottles of New Glaurus beer appeared on the table. "You've got a keyboard for sale?" Katie asked.

Rick nodded, and ran through the opening of "It Don't Matter to Me."

"You a keyboard player?" he asked.

"Yeah. A little." She pulled up a chair.

"Well why don't you join us right here next week. Elsie's got the keyboard in her storage room. I'm sure you'd fit right in with our playing. We're amateurs."

Tom laughed. "That's a polite word for it."

Rick played the opening of "Love Grows" and told Katie, "Let's form a band, you, me, and Tom." She and Tom laughed, but Rick could see in their eyes that they would do it.

Tom set his old acoustic guitar aside, took a slug of beer, and said, "I've had my eye on an electric bass in Bay Pawn for a long time. It's a knock-off of a Gibson Firebird, I think. If Katie is taking us electric, I need an electric bass." He grinned at Rick. "Since I know you're going to want to play lead guitar with a big shiny Stratocaster, we might as well make the change right now."

Rick couldn't suppress his smile. He'd already been over to Bayfield Pawn twice looking at electric guitars, and they had an old Stratocaster there that he could afford. "Let's do it," Rick said.

Katie turned out to be pretty good. She could only play a few chords and a little melody here and there, but she had a perfect sense of timing and was willing to work hard, to take the music seriously. Her voice was beautiful. The second week in August, Rick gave her a couple of his own compositions and she made the vocals sound better than they had ever sounded in his own mind.

Their audience was growing. And Elsie's veranda wasn't really the right place for the now-electric trio that Katie had named Evermore, after her art gallery.

"I need to close up at six and get home," Elsie told them. "You folks can keep playing, but I've got to close at six. I'm too old to work until eight o'clock at night."

So they moved to the veranda in front of Katie's art gallery. And changed to playing Saturday and Sunday evenings instead of Wednesdays, since that's when most of the tourists were on Madelaine Island. Katie hired Eleanor Miller's daughter to mind sales in the Gallery while she was playing and singing. Rick liked the smiles and applause. Some evenings people set up their beach chairs in the empty lot across the street and stayed for their whole set. Only Tom wasn't happy with the new arrangement. He didn't say anything, but his bass playing was sloppy and Rick could tell he really didn't care that much about the music. But Rick did care—about the music, about the applause, about Katie's smile. They kept going.

By the end of August, the Friday night crowds were sitting on the curb on both sides of the street and some people set up their beach chairs on the sidewalk. In preparation for Labor Day weekend, Katie painted some posters and put them up down at the ferry dock. She rented lawn chairs from Everett's lumber and had Elsie prepare to cater drinks and sandwiches. Even before they started playing, people had filled up the street in front of her Gallery. The weather was perfect. They played through their entire repertoire, twice, while Venus glowed in the evening sky. Rick knew he was playing better than he ever had, Tom's bass-playing wasn't much, but nobody seemed to care, because it was Katie the crowd loved. Her voice soared.

That music, on that summer night, was the best thing to happen in La Pointe for a long time.

Rick pulled at the sleeping bag in his fitful sleep. A phantom shape rose up from an Indian grave at his feet. The specter dodged past him and, with simian speed, climbed the trunk of a pine tree and disappeared. The sound of clawed feet going up the outside wall of the cabin woke him. Then there were soft cat footfalls on the metal roof. In the distance, two cats screamed at each other.

Goddamned cats. Rick pulled on clothes and boots and clicked on the flashlight, but its faint glow was nearly useless. He scrabbled around in the grey steel storage locker and found a box with two D-Cells left in it. Rick changed batteries and the light came on strong and bright. He pushed the stuff back into the locker. One small box was surprisingly heavy. Inside it was a shiny black Smith and Wesson 9mm automatic and a box of 50 Magtech rounds.

"Dave's old pistol." Rick grinned. "I remember this thing." He pulled the action back, checked the chamber, then loaded eight of the heavy cartridges into the magazine. He snapped the magazine into the handle of the gun, cocked it, and put the box back on the shelf. "I'm going after those stinking cats right now!"

The pines were motionless black shadows in the deepening fog. Nothing moved. He spent a long time creeping around the forest but saw nothing. He returned to the cabin and stoked up the fire in the fire pit.

"You certainly loved keeping secrets, didn't you, Katie?" Rick muttered to the silence. "You got us our first booking, the Twelfth Avenue Club in Superior. I didn't know you'd been a singer in New York, that you kept in touch with your agent, Sid Lieberman, who you talked into helping a start-up band like ours get our first gigs. And that winter you and Lieberman got us studio time at Northern Recording in Minneapolis. So much I never knew about you, girl. Why'd you keep it hidden from me?" Rick shrugged. "Doesn't really matter now, all that's in the past."

Rick went inside and dug through his duffel bag and pulled out three vinyl LPs in worn covers. "I brought these along, thinking I could live here in the cabin, start my life over, maybe play these records from time to time and think about the good times. Live the simple life." He stared at the cover of *Deep Water*, their first album, as he muttered, "I thought we were really on our way when we recorded this one. But we weren't."

The cover photo was taken in La Pointe, on Second Street. Rick and Katie and Tom leaned against Tom's old pickup. Behind the truck was a corner of Katie's gallery, bright with fresh paint. *I look like I'm angry, Tom is trying to look cool, but I can see he's nervous. Katie? Well, she looks like she belongs on record covers. And maybe she did.*

Rick took all three albums out to his chair by the fire. He stared at the worn cardboard covers in the firelight. "But the good old days weren't so good, were they?"

The back cover of *Deep Water* had a smaller photo with Katie center, in paisley-patched jeans and Mexican peasant blouse, her arms around Rick and Tom, the three of them laughing in the sunshine. Tom's moustache looked so '70s. Rick flipped the record jacket over and read the familiar text. It seemed like a voice from another age—earnest statements about the purity of music and peace and love, like the Age of Aquarius had never died. He grinned. "I'll always have an image of this record jacket covered with the cheap pot we used to smoke, Katie rolling joint after joint in Zig-Zags.

"I guess these old records don't have the magic to turn bad memories to good." He tossed *Deep Water* onto the fire. The cardboard lit and the photo burned away; the vinyl smoked toxic black smoke then curled into a grey knot in the embers. *I was pretty proud of that record. Three weeks of recording and mixing. Sales were good. I was elated. But being on the road, trying to write new music and play old music. It wore me out.*

Katie was in the center of the cover of their second album, *Blue-Grey Eyes*. Rick remembered her amazingly beautiful blue-grey eyes. In the cover photo Rick was beside her, holding his guitar. Tom frowned in the background. Rick tossed the album on the fire without even glancing at the playlist. *Those songs were crap. We knew it then; I know it now.*

The third album, *Superior*, had a darker cover. Just him and Katie. Tom was gone. The music was different too—a heavily produced sound, two sidemen and a couple of session players. By then they were playing bigger clubs: in Duluth, Minneapolis, Madison. Rick studied his and Katie's face in the worn record album jacket. *Neither of us are smiling. Flash clothes and hair. Drinking from morning until night as the limousine drove us from this place to that. A blur of faces and places.* For the record jacket photo, the photographer had told them to try to look mysterious. *We tried, but mostly we just looked tired.* He read the names of some of the tracks on the album. *Some pretty good stuff, despite the booze and the drugs, but not good enough to make us stars.*

Onto the fire it went.

The fatigue of memory forced him into the cold cabin, where he pulled the sleeping bag around him and dreamed of the first time he and Katie had made love, right here in this cabin. There had been magic in the air that sparkling autumn afternoon. They'd sailed out and spent the afternoon exploring the tiny island hand in hand. They'd reveled in the scent of pine in the sweet breeze and the great blue-grey expanse of Lake Superior, as though the world was newly minted and just for them. They'd shared secrets the way people do in the first flame of being in love, feeling that naive intimacy that only occurs once in a love affair.

Later, as they sat by the fire, he played a little Dylan on his acoustic guitar.

"A sad song, about a guy leaving . . ." Katie said when he finished. "You played an upbeat song the first time I met you. 'Love Grows.' and not long after that you said we should form a band. You sounded awfully confident."

"I am," Rick said. "I figure anything I put my mind to, I can do."

"That's a bit egotistical, isn't it? Does it include manipulating people?"

He didn't answer.

"Sorry," she said. "I'm sometimes a little tactless." She put her hand on his arm. "I'm probably just projecting my faults onto you."

He offered her a beer, but she lit a joint, took a hit, and offered it to him. "Play that new song you were just working on. I think I've got some lyrics that are perfect for it."

Later, as the fire burned low and Cassiopeia and Ursa Minor made their slow dance around Polaris, he told her he loved her and she said the same to him.

They made love again in their sleeping bags.

Late that night, Rick got up to put out the oil lamp.

"I need to ask," Rick said, sliding back into warmth. "Are you and Tom . . . ?"

"Tom? No," she told him. "Tom's cool, but he's not for me. He didn't seem offended when I told him no."

"Your voice is wonderful," Rick said. "But I'm sure you know that. Have you sung before?"

She did not answer.

The tours wore them out, mind and body. Rick was drinking daily to ease the tension. Bayfield Apple Festival was the breaking point. Two years, ten tours, three albums, and he and Katie—and probably everyone else—knew the band was no longer on the way up. They were just hanging on; soon it would be downhill. The crowds in the bars were thinner. Most of their old venues had shifted to recorded disco music.

"Why'd you book us into Applefest, Sid?" Rick had shouted over the phone. "It's a step back, not a step forward."

"You guys are hometown favorites, Rick. Make it feel reminiscent."

At Applefest they were the headliners. But their playing was the worst it had been since they started. They stumbled through two short sets, after which Rick stomped off stage. There was a small wave of puzzled applause, the audience clearly disappointed, and then nothing.

Backstage, Dave, his wife Angela, and her ten-year-old son were waiting. Dave stuck out his hand and Rick shook it. "Great to see you again, Rick," Dave beamed. Angela tried to hug him but Rick dodged her. He ignored the kid.

"Hiya Dave." Rick grimaced. "Good to see you. Not our best tonight . . ."

"It was great," the kid said shyly. Angela thrust him toward Rick. "Jason would like to have your autograph, Rick."

Rick held his temper in check, grabbed the notepad, and scrawled his signature across it.

"Thanks, guys," Rick choked out. His anger and embarrassment was rising almost higher than his ability to control it. He would not be able to sit at a plastic table with Dave and his wife and kid, talking about old times and how the kid was doing in school. He mumbled an excuse and practically ran to his Winnebago.

Dave's face turned red. Without a word, he took his son's hand and dragged him out of the big tent, his wife trotting behind him.

In his Winnebago, Rick drank a quarter of a bottle of bourbon fast, then lit a joint and smoked it hard. But nothing seemed to soothe the raging ocean of anger and guilt and frustration that lay inside him.

Katie burst into his RV. "You bastard! Your prima donna bullshit is out of control. You insulted the audience with your bad playing and you insulted your old friend and his family just now!"

Rick's face reddened. He slammed the bottle down on the table and shouted, "Get out."

She stood her ground. "You're making this tour fail. You know that. Our second record bombed, our third's not doing so well. We need for this tour to succeed, but so far we haven't half-filled any club we've played."

"Blaine and Hal need to time to get into the groove," Rick said in a menacing tone. "New sidemen always do."

"Those guys don't have our sound, Rick. You shouldn't have fired Tom . . ."

"He was holding us back."

"My singing will carry us . . ." Katie told him.

"So now you're the star!" shouted Rick. "You're the goddam star. Well it was my original music and my arrangement of those cover songs that put this band on the map . . ."

"But that was then, and people want something new," she snarled back.

"You told the sidemen to put that Captain and

Tennille crap in our second set tonight, didn't you?" Rick screamed at her. "I decide the setlists, not you, and not the sidemen, got it?"

"'Love Will Keep Us Together' was the most requested song—"

"I don't give a shit! This is my band and I decide on the setlist!" Rick screamed. "Don't go behind my back!" He shoved her out the door, then closed and locked it.

"I don't need this," he muttered, glaring around at the bleak RV. He grabbed the bourbon and drank.

I may have to fire her too, he thought.

Poor lost Tom. I chewed him up and spit him out. I told everyone I just wanted the band to be better, but inside I knew I was blaming Tom for things that weren't his fault. I wanted to push hard, play more complex stuff, not just what the bar owners thought customers wanted. Tom never cared what we played. He just liked playing. He wanted things to stay the same. Just as they were in the beginning, back in La Pointe, playing just for the fun of it. Drinking beer in the sunshine of long summer days, living the laid-back island life, taking each day as it came. But that wasn't enough for me.

Smoke from the fire made his eyes sting.

After they'd finished their final set at the Pandora Club in Madison, Rick had asked Tom to stay a moment. The rest of the band had already gone. Just Rick and Tom on a bare stage. A single spotlight remained on, aimed at the microphone Katie used.

Rick had his always-present bottle of Jack Daniels in his hand. The hot burn of the liquor would help him say what he needed to say.

"I'll be straight with you, Tom. You're just not cutting it. You don't learn our new music; you just fall back on the old shuffle, the old progressions. You're not in time with the beat, and to top it off, you stop playing for a bar or two sometimes. What the hell are you trying to do?"

Tom looked out into the darkness of the empty bar. "Artistic pauses, like Entwhistle or Jones. It gives the music a little bit looser feel, you know?"

"No, I don't know." Rick's anger had begun its long slow burn again. He slugged down more bourbon to soothe the flames, but it didn't help. He knew it wasn't just Tom's inept playing that was driving him crazy. It was all of it: a surly Katie, music that people didn't want to hear, half-full houses, daily phone calls from Sid Leiberman.

"I don't need all this hassle," Rick said. "And I'm pretty sure we don't need you."

"Maybe you don't," Tom said quietly. "And I'm more than sure I don't need you, this band, all this crap."

Rick held his anger back with great effort. "Think over what you're saying, because if you leave now, I am not hiring you back."

"That suits me fine," Tom said. He picked up his bass, put it in its case, and walked into the darkness offstage, his footsteps hollow on the bare wood floor. His footsteps paused, and from the darkness Tom asked, "Is it still fun, Rick?" Then he was gone.

Rick sat there for a while, a black and white figure in the single spotlight.

"Well, it's his choice," Rick told the emptiness. "Blaine can cover bass. Hal's good on the keyboard. Let superstar Katie just do vocals."

Rick picked up his old Gibson acoustic and played a little bit of their bestseller, "Haunted by You," but it wasn't enjoyable. He tried the opening bars of "Blue-Grey Eyes," but it sounded empty too. He put the guitar down and took his bottle to his silent hotel room.

The next day Tom phoned me, wanted the money the band owed him. I explained Lieberman was holding all receipts until the end of the tour. I had nothing to give him. I was borrowing money from the roadies for my daily bottle of Jack Daniels. He said he just needed enough to buy a truck, some tools, go back to being a handyman in La Pointe. But I couldn't give him anything.

Rick got up and went to the window. Fog lay along the ground. A manlike shape stood near a tree not thirty feet away. Rick grabbed the flashlight, stuck the gun in his pocket, and rushed out into the cold night. The flashlight's weakening beam was becoming useless, but Rick thought he saw Tom's mustard colored Carhardtt coveralls, his blue Pendleton shirt, his long blond hair in a ponytail.

"Tom?" Rick rasped. The figure seemed to fade back into the blackness between the trees. He advanced, but the wraith had faded to darkness. "Tom? Is that you?" Rick called to the silent forest. "What are you doing out here?"

There was silence, then the yowl of a cat. "Damned cats!" Rick shouted. He blundered on through the forest, determined to shoot any cat he saw. Or any ghost.

Ahead, the pines thinned out near the edge of the bluff overlooking the lake. Rick reached the edge of the woods and stared out over an unbroken layer of fog on top of the lake water, white and flat to the horizon. An irrational part of his mind told him he could walk out on it, like ice. Walk all the way to the mainland.

He laughed, a strange sound, answered by the mournful yowl of a cat.

He hurried back to the cabin, locked the door behind him, and sat on the couch with his feet propped up on his toolbox, bottle and gun at hand.

Evermore's sound did not improve. They tried new stuff, old stuff; nothing was working. The sidemen couldn't find their groove, and since Rick and Katie were not speaking to each other, they had no help trying to learn the music and fit themselves into the band. Audiences were not happy. The Night Owl Club canceled them the day before they were scheduled to play.

"They don't think you're going to bring in a crowd, so they won't pay your fee," Lieberman told Rick in his daily phone call. Rick hung up and opened a fresh bottle of bourbon and sat in his silent hotel room all afternoon, drinking steadily. Eventually he staggered to the bed and fell into a drunken sleep as night enveloped the city.

At noon the next day there was a knock on his hotel door. Rick struggled up out of his stupor. "Time to get on the road," Kevin the roadie said from the corridor. Rick got the door open and stumbled back to bed. Kevin set two bottles of Jack Daniels on the table.

"Limo's waiting." Kevin said, picking up Rick's suitcase, still packed, and grinned. "Makes it easier if you never unpack, right?" As the door swung shut, Kevin said cheerily, "By the way, Katie quit this morning."

Rick unscrewed the top of one of the bottles and took a solid slug of whiskey.

That night at the Center Stage Club in Prairie Du Chien, Rick, drunk to the point he could barely stand, tried and failed to play their opening number, finally threw down his guitar, and staggered off stage. The audience was in an uproar. The club manager offered patrons free drinks and shouted at Hal and Blaine to play something.

"You bastards are going to play tonight until ten, and without that drunk! And when you leave here tonight, I never want to see any of you again!"

Rick woke in a hotel room with someone pounding on the door. He let Kevin in. "I got to get out of here, man; cops are onto me. I need that money you owe me." Rick stared at him, his hangover pounding. Kevin went through Rick's billfold and left. The hotel phone buzzed. It was the manager telling him to vacate his room immediately. They had phoned the police, but if Rick left quietly now, they would not press charges.

"What charges?"

"Possession of narcotics." The phone went dead.

Rick scrambled into his clothes, down the elevator, and out through the restaurant kitchen. Outside in the cold wind he accosted a young woman.

"What town is this?"

"Duluth."

Rick had forty dollars in his pants pockets.

A dozen cats were yowling and screeching now. Rick's temper exploded. He grabbed the gun and the flashlight and raced out through the pine forest, chasing flitting black shadows. He fired while he dodged between trees, oblivious of scrapes and scratches. Finally he slowed, out of breath. The cats had disappeared. He walked forward. Where the pine trees ended the flat plain of fog stretched out to a hazy horizon. A thin, black wraith seemed to be out there, running along the top of the fog. Rick fired at it until the gun clicked empty.

He looked down. Ten feet in front of him and thirty feet down in deep fog was a white oval coffin. Rick backed away in horror. It took a moment for him to comprehend that he was seeing the white hull of the *Lucy* in the hidden cove. He was standing not ten feet from the cliff edge of the cove. He backed into a pine tree, then whirled and rushed back to the cabin and locked the door. Then he turned up the oil lamp, took a slug of Jack Daniels, and got out the box of ammo.

The light was dim, the oil lamp almost out of fuel. But there was enough light for him to slide the magazine out of the gun and press one cartridge into it. He stared at his hands; he seemed to have no control over them. He watched his hands slide the magazine into the gun and chamber the single round.

I could end it all now, he thought. *Why not? I don't belong here anymore. I don't belong anywhere.* He did not feel fear, but he did not feel relief either.

Rick looked at the gun for a long time, the yellow light of the oil lamp glowing in the black steel. Then the yellow faded to red, and to darkness.

The lamp ran out of fuel with a low hiss.

He stood in cold darkness for a moment, then refilled the oil lamp, unloaded the gun, and put it back in the cabinet.

The next morning was cold and clear. Rick swallowed aspirin, collected his gear, and clumped down the path to the cove without a backward glance.

At the Madelaine Island marina, Rick moored *Lucy* in her slip, collected his guitar and backpack, and left the key in the slot where Dave always left it.

As he passed the ancient harbormaster's shack, old Bill Anderson stepped out, took his pipe out of his mouth, hacked a wet cough, and told him, "You look like hell, Rick."

Rick paused, shoulders drooping. "Nice to see you too, Bill."

Bill grinned. "I figured it must have been you who took Dave's sloop out. Nobody else knows where Dave leaves the key. Don't matter none. Dave ain't had the *Lucy* out in over a year. Don't know why he keeps paying slip rent."

"Nostalgia, Bill," Rick told him. "Just for old times sake."

"Going back to Duluth today?" Bill asked.

Rick squinted at his Jeep in the parking lot. "No, I'm moving on."

"Where to?"

"East."

Rick moved on before Bill could interrogate him further.

But, in his Jeep, Rick sat staring at the white sailboats in the marina and beyond to Lake Superior's blue-grey water, thinking. *Ghosts own Cat Island now. I always thought of it as my private place, but that's gone, all gone.* Eventually he started the Jeep and motored slowly down Stewart Street, past the old rooming house where he and Tom had shared an apartment in the summer of 1970. He noticed Elsie's store was closed and for rent. Another left onto Second Street, just idling along, the window open to the mild morning. The scent and the color of La Pointe flowed over him like honey.

He was surprised to see the front door of Gallery Evermore open. Big, bright, abstract paintings were on display. He parked and went in.

Katie looked up from the jewelry display case. "Hello Rick."

"You look great," Rick told her.

She stepped around the counter and gave him a perfunctory hug. They stood at arms length and Rick suddenly felt completely at a loss for words. How many nights in that dreary apartment in Duluth had he thought about all the things he wanted to tell her? But now he could think of nothing to say.

"Too bad about Tom," Katie said, taking Rick's hand.

"You've heard from him?"

Katie dropped his hand, frowned, and went to her desk. She handed Rick a clipping from a newspaper.

It was an obituary. *Construction site accident . . . Mr. Thomas Sizemore fell from the roof of the Pointe West Condomium being constructed in west Ashland and died instantly . . . OSHA investigation on-going . . . Mr. Sizemore was unmarried . . . a graduate of Bayfield High School . . . services to be held June 20th . . . .*

Rick felt as though time had stopped. Tears flooded his eyes.

Tom was dead.

"It's a shock," Katie said softly. "We all liked Tom. We didn't treat him as well as we should have . . ."

"You should say, I didn't treat him right . . ." Rick's voice choked. "Tom must have taken a job with some fly-by-night roofing company, and one day the odds caught up with him. Setting roofing shingles he slips and falls off the roof and then he's dead."

"You're not responsible," Rick heard Katie say. "Everyone has to take responsibility for their own life."

"Yeah," Rick said finally. He handed her the clipping. "But if I could do it over again . . ."

"But none of us can, Rick. There's no sense wishing for a past that can never be changed."

"The band was just a dream of mine," Rick said. "I was never that good a musician or a songwriter. You know that. I wish now I'd never started the band. Out at the cabin on Cat Island I was happy." He looked at her. "I was happiest out there with you."

Katie nodded slowly. "Dreams. Sometimes they don't work out. Mine didn't in New York. I thought for a while that maybe in your band I could become a real singer, but . . ." she shook her head. "I'm a better painter than I am a singer. This gallery is what I want to do. Maybe it's my way of living the simple life."

"I just came back from Cat Island," Rick said. "The old cabin."

She smiled a thin smile.

"Maybe we could go out to Cat Island again some time," Rick said. "We had some good times there."

She looked at the empty street in front of the gallery, at her paintings on the wall, at the jewelry in the case. "Let's sit outside in the sunshine," she said.

They pulled plastic chairs up to a round veranda table in the pale island sunshine.

"Feels like the old days," he said. "The veranda in front of Elsie's store. Remember?"

"I remember," Katie said. And after a moment she added, "Elsie died last year."

Rick felt his heart lurch. He felt like his life was being torn out of him piece by piece. "She was . . . kind. I'll miss her."

"I used to send Elsie some money every month while we were on tour. She kept an eye on the gallery for me. I guess I always knew I'd be coming back to it."

There was silence between them for a time. The streaks of cirrus clouds overhead seemed very distant. Even the birds were still.

"I'm sorry," Rick said. "For Tom's death, for all the things that went wrong between us, for a lot of things."

Katie looked away. "As much my fault as yours. That's all in the past."

"We've changed. Both of us," Rick said. She wouldn't meet his eyes for a moment, but when she did, he was once again captured by her remarkable blue-grey eyes.

"We've changed, but what we had is gone, Rick," she said. "You can never go back, not really."

"Maybe we can move ahead . . ."

"No. It's finished. I'm sorry." They looked at each other for a moment as the light faded from his eyes.

"I'm sorry," she repeated, rubbing her hands on the arms of the chair. "I should get back to work."

Rick followed her inside. "Very nice," he said, looking around.

"About a year ago Dave and his family stopped by," Katie said. "I think he said they still keep a boat in the marina here. He owns Payson Construction Company now. Still living in Ashland. They seem to be doing well."

"I'm glad," Rick said. "I haven't seen Dave since. . . Applefest . . . I was a jerk. I was worn out, drunk, stoned . . . ."

Katie turned away, which annoyed him. "It's all in the past, Rick."

"You know, even though there was a lot of bad stuff, a lot of hurt and pain and frustration, sometimes, when the music was right, just for a while, there were some good times."

She smiled. "Yeah, there were some good times. Just for a while."

A woman who had been admiring the artwork through the window came into the gallery. Katie gave her a polite wave. "I need to get back to work," she told Rick softly.

"Yeah," Rick said, "guess I'll be going."

Katie gave him a quick hug. "Take care of yourself."

Rick sat in his Jeep on the short ferry ride to the mainland. In Bayfield he drove the length of Allen Street; then, while he was waiting at the last light at the edge of town, he suddenly jerked the Jeep around in a U-turn and went back to Twelfth Street.

"What'll you give me for this Gibson?" he asked the proprietor of Bay Pawn. The man examined the guitar. "Nice instrument. But . . ." He waved his hand at a half dozen guitars hanging on the display rack. "Best I could do would be two hundred."

"I'll take it," Rick said. He pocketed the cash. There was a liquor store right next to the pawn shop, and

Rick opened its grimy front door. Then he stopped, turned around, and got back in his Jeep.

Stopping drinking will be painful, but I can do it. And it will be painful apologizing to Dave, but I can do that, too.

He'd driven twenty miles down Route 13 before he realized he was whistling "Which Way You Goin', Billy?" He grinned, thinking of the summer of 1970 when he had been happy and all the world seemed to lie before him.

REAPER

Dave stood at the window of the loo looking out over the brick chimneys and tile roofs of central London. He flipped the stub of his cigarette onto the roof below and lit another one. Reaper, his band, had been in the studio all afternoon, and nothing was working. Their old barroom music was weak, and what little new material they had was crap.

It hadn't been that way two months ago when they'd signed with Clive Alston of Arcane Records. They had been playing the Brier pub for over a year and were the most popular band in Clapham, which wasn't saying much since there were only a half dozen garage bands around. But the pop music column in the *Daily Mail* had given them a glowing review, and a rep from Arcane had asked them to meet with Clive Alston, the president.

To their amazement, they'd been offered a contract to do a month's tour of the Midlands as opening act for Foghat. If the tour went well, they would be given studio time to record a single, which Arcane would distribute. For Dave and Colin and Mick and Eric, four kids from Kyrle Road in Clapham, it was a dream come true. Alston didn't tell them he'd only hired them because he needed a band fast—the last one had quit without notice, and the Foghat tour was scheduled to start in a week.

The tour was a high-energy blur. The members of Foghat were aloof, but not the fans, the girls, or the drug dealers. The drinking went on all day and all night, with enough speed to keep Dave and Mick and Eric awake until dawn, when they would board the bus to the next city and do it again. Colin kept to himself. Reaper's playing was good. The energy of being an opening act had pushed them to play better than they ever had before.

And then one day the tour was over, and they all went back to their dingy flats in London. Dave arrived at his flat at six in the evening in the midst of a cold April rain. Patricia, his girlfriend of a year, was drunk and high, chattering continuously about her art and her friend's art, and her friend's friend's art. He eventually exploded. "Shut up for one moment, won't you!" And she did, but their anger soon reasserted itself in an endless argument about nothing and everything. After forty minutes of shouting, Patricia gathered up her things and stormed out.

Which suited Dave fine.

The next day at noon, Reaper assembled in the smaller of the two recording studios Arcane Records owned on Waltham Street.

Mick and Eric were their usual rambunctious selves, while reclusive Colin, clutching his composition book, glared at the sound engineers up in the control box as though they were enemies. Dave tuned his Stratocaster with grim determination.

They had trouble getting started. The fluorescent-lit bareness of the studio was disconcerting after the crowded Brier and the glaring lights of the tour. The four session men—two guitarists, a backup keyboardist, and a backup bassist, were politely distant. Reaper ran through their standard Brier pub set, including their best song: "Stay with Me." But their playing was ragged, and it all sounded amateurish. On break, nobody said anything; the session men avoided eye contact. Then after a few false starts, Reaper tried one of the new tunes Dave and Colin had written while they were on tour. That was even worse. They tried another, then another, with no improvement.

Clive Alston came down from the control booth. "Everything I've heard so far is crap, including the single I've already released for you—"

"Which is doing pretty well," Dave interrupted.

Alston turned on him with a scowl. "Never interrupt me. Do you understand that?"

"Yes, sir," Dave said, shrinking back from the cigar being waved in his face.

"You four were supposed to have been writing great new stuff while you were on tour," Alston continued. "Not just playing with the girls and getting high. So where is it?" He didn't wait for an answer, but turned and stomped back up the stairs to the control booth.

Reaper sweated away at their new material for another two hours with no luck. They tried filling in certain parts with the session men, whose playing was good but didn't fit. Eventually one of the engineers in the control booth switched on the speaker. "Let's take a break, lads."

Dave went off to smoke a cigarette in the third-floor men's room. Leaning out the window, he blew out smoke and watched the May wind whip it away over the roofs. "New material." When they had been playing at the Brier, they'd been king of the hill. They brought the crowds into the pub every Friday and Saturday night, playing covers and a few originals. "Clapham's own!" Arlen the manager used to introduce them. It was all Dave had ever imagined: the deafening ecstasy of the music, the sweating, cheering crowd, the girls, the applause, the drinks, smoking cheap pot in the alley on breaks. It was magic. The *Daily Mail*'s music review called Reaper "Edgy and lyrical. A band to watch. The single 'Stay with Me' is some of the best rock of the year. Its coloration is somehow reminiscent of sixteenth-century madrigals. It's a magical mix."

But now they were just another contract band. Maybe not even that if they didn't come up with a chartable tune in the next couple of days. Pigeons circled and landed on a sooty chimney ten yards away. Dave pointed his hand, thumb cocked, and shot them off their ledge one by one.

"Colin's lyrics are crap; he's too deep into classical nonsense. And I can't get a new melody into my head. All I hear is bloody Foghat and their blues ripoffs. We're nowhere."

Dave stubbed his cigarette out on the tile floor and returned to the empty control room. There were still fifteen minutes left of the thirty-minute break. The engineers were out in the alley smoking dope. The session men sat in their places patiently waiting, doodling bits of tunes on their instruments. Dave studied their faces through the control booth glass. Ordinary guys. You could pass them on the street and never know they'd played, uncredited, on some of the biggest hits on radio. Playing for daily wages. *Maybe that's purity*, Dave thought. *But it's not for me. I'm going to be a star.*

The dark-haired kid on a Rickenbacker guitar was doodling around with the blues shuffle they'd been using on their last disaster of a song. Somebody said something to him. Dave flipped the microphones on so he could hear them. The kid laughed. "You mean, something like this?" He began playing something that was part American surf music, part Welsh folk dance. Dave grabbed a pencil and scribbled some bits of the melody on a scrap of paper and stuffed it in his pocket.

When the band and the engineers returned, they worked on the best of the three new songs for two more hours, making them better, but still far from hit singles.

At six, the engineers told them they were going off duty. Dave, Colin, Mick, and Eric adjourned to the nearest pub.

"All our new songs are crap," Eric said, cheerfully hoisting a pint. "And our playing is absolute shite."

"Shut up, you bloody wog!" Dave roared at him.

After two pints, Dave took the tube to his flat, got out his Martin D-28, and worked through the melody he'd heard the kid playing. On a blank sheet of paper, he noted down transitions and chords, and added a melodic line and repeats. But most importantly, he emphasized the hypnotic backbeat that had drawn him to it in the first place.

The next day at the studio, Dave gave Colin, Eric, Mick, and the session men copies of his handwritten notes. Colin scrabbled through his composition book and began adding lyrics. Eric and Mick started playing the bass line and percussion, with a session man filling in for Colin on keyboard and one guitarist filling in for Dave, who went up to the control booth. Dave studied the dark-haired kid's face for signs of recognition, but there were none. After Colin had some lyrics sketched out, Dave came back, and Reaper played it through with the session men and then without them. Then they played it through again. A few more tries, and it was sounding good.

In two hours, they had a rough cut on tape. Colin's title was "No Time for Us." Melody by Dave, lyrics by Colin. At lunchtime, with a rough cut of the tape in hand, the four of them trooped up to Alston's office and played it for him. When it ended, Alston came around his desk and shook Dave's hand. "That's what I'm looking for—hit material. I knew you had it in you." He didn't shake hands with the rest of them. "You guys take the rest of the day off."

Eric and Mick bolted down the stairs, out the back door, and down the street to the pub.

Colin was waiting for Dave outside. The wind between the dirty brick walls of the alley was cold, and there were spits of rain in the air.

"You waiting for someone?" Dave asked Colin, who was standing just outside the door. "Bloody cold out here."

"Now what do we do?" Colin asked Dave.

"What do you mean?" Dave said.

Colin turned up his collar against the wind. "Bloody cold. It's April and still..."

"So what's your worry now, mate?" Dave snapped. "Come to the pub; I'll buy you a pint. But let's get out of this wind."

"We may not want to work with these session men for a while," Colin said. He turned profile to Dave. "I know you didn't write the music for 'No Time for Us.' You cribbed it off those session men."

Dave stamped his feet to warm them. "Well it's got my name on it now. I didn't hear you, or the session men, complaining back in the studio. We've given Alston the hit he wanted from us, and everything's cool. Those session men aren't going to complain."

Colin faced Dave. "That's what I'm talking about, Dave. You going to steal another melody for our next hit song?"

"Would you rather be back at the Brier?" snarled Dave, stepping up to confront Colin. "No recording contract, playing for ten quid a night, no future. Is that what you want? Well, I want a hell of a lot more than to be some bar band in Clapham." Dave turned to go, and Colin grabbed his elbow. Dave shook his hand off.

"What I'm saying," Colin said to Dave's glare, "is that we'd better not work with those particular session men for a while."

"So we tell Alston to hire some new ones." Dave shrugged.

"We need to make our own music. I do anyway. Session men around all the time, the glare of those lights in the studio, the engineers up behind their glass windows like vultures. The studio drives all the creativity out of my head. I can write good stuff. I just need to get away for a while."

"Alright," Dave said slowly. "Let's try it. Get away, be on our own, see if we can write music or not." Dave squared his shoulders. "Alston is all smiles right now, so it's the right time to get him to let us go somewhere off by ourselves. And I know the place. There's a mobile recording studio there already. Foghat just finished up an album down there. The bass man told me about it."

"Where?" Colin said. His eagerness seemed pathetic to Dave.

"Farley Manse in Wiltshire. Two hours down the A2606. It's a crumbling old mansion. But the Foghat bass player says it's great. Those country places can work their magic. Fleetwood Mac in 1970. Their *Kiln House* album was recorded outside the studio. And Led Zeppelin's *ZoSo* album was done at Headley Grange. Now it's our turn."

Colin's expression had become withdrawn. "We've got to try..."

Dave shook his shoulders. "Try, hell. We'll succeed!"

"I just want time and space to write lyrics that mean something. Something like John Clare—"

"Alright, alright," Dave interrupted.

"I'll buy you a pint," Colin said, brightening, but Dave shook his head.

"Not now. Alston's still up in his office, and I'm going to pay him a visit. Get this operation moving as soon as possible."

And so two caravans full of band members, roadies, groupies, instruments, and recording gear wound up a narrow track under alders dripping with the afternoon's rain, and through the stone arch that fronted ancient Farley Manse. They parked on an unkempt lawn, and people spilled out of the cramped vans.

"Look!" Sheila, one of the groupies who seemed to have attached herself to Mick, pointed at the western sky, where a rainbow arced between clouds.

Dave pushed open the massive oak door and went inside. "Need some lights in here!"

The roadies got to work setting up the quiet generator they'd brought and running cables and lights into the crumbling ruin of a mansion. They wrestled a small refrigerator into the ancient kitchen and filled it with three cases of Brown's Bitter Ale.

People roamed at will through the great room, its vaulted ceiling hung with tattered banners, the leaded glass windows so obscured by vines as to allow only a wan glow of sunlight into the room. A mixed bag of furniture was scattered about.

Dave went up a curving wooden stair to the second floor and found a corridor between surprisingly small bedrooms, some unfurnished.

Eric and Mick clowned with the groupies in the great room. Colin wandered his own silent way, then reappeared in the great room just as Dave came up the stone steps from the wine cellar. "Great cellar. No wine, but arched ceilings, old wooden table, and the silence is almost tangible."

As soon as the roadies had instruments, amps, and recording equipment set up, Reaper ran through the suite of oldies and a couple of forgettable but original songs they'd been using to open every Friday night at the Brier. It sounded great.

"Acoustics are perfect!" Eric shouted, hurling his drumsticks up at the age-darkened pennants hanging from the ceiling vault. "Now, where's the nearest pub?"

"Not yet!" Dave shouted at him. "We need to talk about our plan for this week."

"I know your plan," Mick said. "You expect us to lie about this rotting castle looking for magic in the candlelight, all that bloody Fairport Convention stuff. We don't need that, man—we're a rock band, we're stars. We should be back in London pushing for every gig we can get, not down here listening to the music of the spheres."

"More gigs won't help us," Colin said reasonably from where he sat behind his keyboard. "We need new music to keep our name alive. Top 40 has a short memory. You heard Alston."

"Give us the music and we'll play it," Mick said, laying his bass guitar down and grabbing a bottle of beer. "I figured you'll need this evening to get the new stuff organized. We'll go at it fresh tomorrow." He rose and signaled Eric. "I saw a pub down the lane a bit. We'll walk there."

"Not yet," Dave repeated, staring Eric and Mick down. Pamela passed beer bottles around to ease the tension. A hash pipe circulated. Everyone settled themselves on the two ancient sofas. The age-rippled glass in the windows turned the sunset light gold and purple.

Sheila seated herself on the floor by the low wooden table, opened a foil packet, took something out, and held it up near the three candles on the table. "Orange sunshine, just in from San Francisco." The orange rectangle in her palm glowed as though lit with fire.

"The doors of perception," Colin said.

Eric winked at Mick, who grinned. "Doors of perception my arse," Eric said, giving Sheila's right boob a friendly squeeze. "That's twelve hours of gods and demons. Not for me. I like me alcohol with a light touch of speed to keep me going, right Sheila luv?"

"Don't jar me arm while I'm breaking this LSD into right-sized pieces."

She laid them on a small Nepalese tray, popped one into her mouth, and washed it down with a swig of Brown's Bitter. Then she passed the tray to Dave, who took one, and Colin, who took one. Mick and Eric passed.

"Before we enter the empyrean realm, let me remind you of a couple of things," Dave said.

"Gawd," Mick said, slugging down beer. "A commercial."

"We've been on tour," Dave told them, "which went well. We played our pub music, which is pretty weak. But Alston released 'Stay with Me' as a single, which got into the Top 40. Now Alston's about to release our second single, 'No Time for Us,' which should do pretty well too—"

"So we're sitting on top of the world," Eric crowed. "We should be touring—"

"No we shouldn't," Dave snapped at him. "Two hit singles and a one-month tour just barely gets us in the door. Now we need an album, new music, strong music, to take us through the door."

"So?" Mick snorted. "Colin writes the lyrics, you write the melody, we all record it. It's dead simple, man." He nudged Sheila to hand him another beer.

Dave looked around at all their faces starting to shift and flow as the acid began to affect his perception. "We need magical music," Dave articulated with difficulty. "And we won't find that in the studio. This place will help us find it." He peered out the leaded glass window at the tangled lawn in evening light. Several fireflies winked. "I'm asking you guys to do the best you can. That's all."

Colin looked pensively at the vaulted ceiling; the dusty remains of flags hung in tatters. There were a half dozen framed portraits high on the wall, darkened past recognition. "You need to believe that spirits exist in the stone and the mortar and the timbers of this ancient estate...they will fire our imaginations, lead to great music, show us visions..."

Eric and Mick traded glances. Mick downed his lager, stood up, and stomped around the tangle of cables, amps, recording machines, instruments. "That's all shite! We don't need some ghostly inspiration—we're rockers, man."

Eric stood up too. "I don't favor sitting in the gloom waiting for visions. I'm with Mick. There's a pub down the lane, and I'm going to go drink a pint or three among real people. That's where you get inspired."

He and Mick banged out the door. The roadies and groupies carefully avoided eye contact with Colin or Dave.

"Let them go," Dave told them all. "Go write some lyrics, Colin." Colin, always too docile, slowly ascended the curving wooden staircase in silence.

"You lot entertain yourselves this evening, but I don't want a racket," Dave told the rest of them. He picked up his acoustic guitar and a bottle of Brown's Bitter and went down the stone stair to the wine cellar. Sheila followed with a tray of lit candles and left them on the table then went back up the steps, her bare feet silent on the worn stone.

It was cool and quiet in the wine cellar. Several torn velour chairs stood along a wall facing a decrepit wooden table. Dave settled into a chair, put

his Martin D-28 on the chair beside him, and lit a
Players. He slowly drank his beer and smoked one
cigarette, then another, and watched the movement
of ceiling cobwebs in the candles' rising heat. Eric's
words stayed in Dave's mind: *We should be touring.*
Once, in a heated moment backstage after a concert
in Manchester, Eric had shouted at Dave, *We're a club
band, man! We'll never be anything else. We need to
make the most of what we are, not spend time trying to
be something we're not. Sorry man, but you and Colin
aren't Page and Plant.*

Shadows moved in the dust, ghosts in the gloom.
Slow footsteps came down the stone stairs. Sheila
on sandaled feet. She handed him a fresh beer and
disappeared up the stair.

Dave picked up the silky Martin guitar and laid
it against his chest. The acid was playing melodies
he could not quite hear. Very faint liquid azure and
carnelian colors ran down the tile walls, so faint he
could barely see them, but their motion caught his
eye.

*What did Colin say on the drive down: We are going
into the deep country, the ancient forest. The great god
Pan's country. Keats once wrote: "Pan, dread opener of
mysterious doors to universal knowledge."*

Dave pulled a joint out from among the cigarettes
in the Players box, lit it from a candle, and took a long
satisfying hit. "Play your syrinx for me, Pan. Give me
a melody."

But there was only silence.

He languorously sipped his beer, floating on the warm feeling of limitless time, without deadlines, without Alston shouting at him. The fetid air seemed to ripple as his gaze drifted around the dark corners of the cellar.

In a low corner beyond the heavy oak table, he thought he saw something move.

"Great god Pan and your nymphs," he said aloud, "show yourself."

The ripples of darkness seemed to form a face, slowly but endlessly changing, human and not human, bearded, smiling an unwelcoming smile. His heart thudded slowly and steadily as he watched. But the more he concentrated, the more the image slid away. He looked away, and when he looked back, there was only darkness beneath the table.

Dave opened one of the composition books on the table and began scrawling music across the lines, anything that crossed his mind. They were unhappy notes, full of fear and anger. He saw himself, a small boy in their bleak cold house in Clapham, his life bounded by fear and anger and unhappiness. He wrote the notes out, page after page, until they stopped coming and he laid the pen down and went upstairs to his tiny room to sleep, a sleep troubled by psychedelic dreams. Outside his window, Mars was rising in the night sky.

He dreamed, or maybe not, that he wakened and walked down through the empty manse, outside across the unkempt paddock to woods' edge. Fireflies glittered across the lawn. And then he was in his bed, leaning forward to look out the open window at smoky Mars low in the southern sky.

Eric's banging on his drum kit wakened Dave. No clock in the room and Dave didn't own a watch, but the sun was half down the sky—so afternoon. Dave pulled himself together and went downstairs.

Colin caught him on the stairs. "I went out into the sunshine across the sward to the woods." Colin's eyes seemed dull, nearly closed. He spoke with a drawl. "Dragonflies are there. Wings of emerald and carnelian and...and..." He stopped, as though he were reciting something and had forgotten a line. "A great oak tree has died and fallen at the edge of the field. A dryad is there, almost visible, not quite, just iridescent shimmer..." Words failed him again, and he stood motionless, a wax figure on the stair, while others moved about the great room setting up for the day.

"I've seen her too," Dave told him. "Or maybe it was Pan himself. In the wine cellar—no, in the woods. The acid pulled me there, late last night. There were fireflies everywhere. The woods was pitch black. I stopped at the oak tree. And after a while I realized I was hearing amidst the night sounds, I was hearing a soft voice singing. I felt a presence, a girl's voice I could not quite hear, singing. And then I saw her, or something, floating amongst the branches above my head—a slim girl with slow beating dragonfly wings..."

Colin stared at him, then continued down the stair.

Dave walked past the people in the great room. "Not yet, people." He went out the heavy oak front door that would not close completely, across a weedy lawn under pale sunshine and a skim of cirrus clouds, through the open stone arch into the adjoining paddock. He walked across a field of rippling yellow; dragonflies flitted. In the shade of the woods, it was cooler. A breeze whispered. He was standing beside an ancient rotting oak. The grey pattern of the ancient tree's bark drew his eye; the air in front of the tree shimmered. His eye was drawn out to the sunny field and lost in sun dazzle. When he looked back, the bark was unmoving. He stood, intensely aware of the presence of the tree, the rustle of its leaves overhead, the dappling shade around his feet in the fallen leaves and mosses. Air shimmered again.

"There is a magic," he said, the words coming into his mind as though someone was reading them to him and he was speaking them. He stared at the bark of the oak tree and saw it was alive.

"I want..." He stopped, somehow aware that the wraith in his presence already knew what he wanted. After a time, he went back inside. But he waved the rest of them away. "I'm...not able to play right now. In the cellar, I wrote some melodies—work with them." Dave tossed his composition book down, went upstairs to his room, and lay half asleep and half awake. Acid dreams carried him on and on. Afternoon passed, and night.

Next day about noon, Dave felt up to trying to play. The recording men had their gear operating, Eric was pounding away on his drum kit, and Mick worked a bass line. There was much laughter amongst the roadies and the groupies smoking dope at the end of the room.

Dave tuned his Stratocaster and played a few sequences on it, then nodded at Colin. New music had been written out and set in front of each of them. Colin had arranged the ragged notes Dave had scribbled out into four songs and put lyrics to them. It took them all a long time to warm up to it. But Mick and Eric for once weren't disruptive. They worked away until the light began to fade outside the tall windows. Eric threw his drumsticks against the wall, grabbed Mick, and banged out the door and down the lane.

Dave asked the sound man if he'd gotten it. After a bit, he had the best of it cut together, and he played it back while Dave and Colin and the girls lay on the rotting sofas drinking beer and passing a joint.

"It's a start," Dave said, knowing it really was not any good. He gathered up a beer and his acoustic guitar, slipped a sliver of orange sunshine into his mouth, and retired to the wine cellar.

"It's here," he whispered. "The magic is here. It's got to be." He realized he was staring at some translucent thing hovering high in a dark corner of the arched stone ceiling. Fairy wings were beating slowly in the shadows of the vaulted ceiling, almost invisible against the dark staining of centuries of candle smoke. After a time, he realized there was nothing there but the slow wave and ripple of a drape of cobweb.

"Dryad," Dave said. Colin had talked once about dryads, the spirits of trees but also of music, Pan's companions.

Dave saw Colin descend slowly into the wine cellar, not sure if he was real or illusion. "I saw something..." Dave told him in a voice he didn't recognize as his own. He had difficulty focusing his eyes on Colin's rotund shape, which tended to strobe away to right or left. "I saw something," Dave repeated, struggling up from the chair, his beer slopping on the worn tile floor. "Something...fantastical. Magic."

"Yes," Colin said. "I have lyrics..."

Dave followed Colin up the stone staircase to the cathedral-like great room, where they sprawled on the two sofas, facing each other across a table littered with beer bottles, pot, guttered candles, pills of rainbow colors, and a dirty hand-mirror smeared with white dust.

The melody Dave had written out lay on the table. He picked it up, picked up his acoustic guitar, and began playing. Colin's lyrics of love and loss, hate, revenge, and fear lay across the music like a bloody stain.

But the music flowed, and the words fit. Dave clicked on a tape recorder, and Colin and he sang badly, but they got the lyrics onto tape. He changed from acoustic to his Strat and played the melody through several times while he and Colin sang all the lyrics through once. Then he set the guitar aside, rewound the tape, and played it back. It was very ragged, but the song was haunting. After a while, he roused himself to turn off the tape recorder.

"Is it night or day?" Dave asked Colin, who was already dozing. "I need to rest," Dave said and went up to his room. The dreams persisted. Angry images, fear and frustration—his sleep was not restful.

The next day, Dave pulled himself into consciousness and went downstairs. There was no coffee, so he took a beer to the ruined sofa in the great room and drank while he sat in a stupor.

He heard sounds from upstairs. He went to the front door and peered out. It looked like late afternoon. "Time to roust Eric and Mick out of the pub, find Colin, and try to get this music to work." He made his way up the curving staircase, following the faint sounds. In the upstairs corridor, only one door was closed. As Dave approached, his footsteps clacking on the worn wooden floor, the sounds stopped.

He knocked on the door of the room Colin had selected, then went in. "Sorry, I..."

Colin sat at a table he'd pushed up to the window, which stood open. Papers and books were scattered all about. The bed was neatly made. A bottle of Bushmills stood on the desk. Colin's eyes were swollen; his nose was running. He looked away and covered his face with a handkerchief. Dave looked at the floor uncomfortably. The acid in his head seemed to have dissipated, leaving the world monochrome.

"We need to work on the music," Dave said, embarrassed at seeing Colin like this.

Colin sat with his head in his hands. "Not now," he said.

The window was open, but the room still seemed airless. Dave thought of Colin's tiny attic room at his mum's house in Clapham.

"I was happier before we started all this," Colin said to the open window. "After school up in my room I'd read the poets, doze, dream..."

"Well, maybe you can turn those dreams into lyrics," Dave assayed. "This retreat was your idea. An escape from all the jumble in London. This is what you wanted..."

Colin's deep frown drilled Dave. "Yeh. I got what I asked for. But it's not what I want."

"What do you want?"

"To write poetry. Not this crap!" Colin slapped his ever-present composition book. "Rock lyrics are crap."

"It will take us some time to get used to these poetic lyrics," Dave said in a placating tone. "Maybe you should write some simpler stuff. Like you used to write when we were playing at the old Brier. Everybody liked that stuff."

Colin was not to be placated. "They were drunk. And they liked anything that had enough beat so they could dance. They couldn't care less about lyrics."

"But 'Stay with Me' took off," Dave persisted. "You wrote the lyrics. We played it at the Brier. People loved it. I'm sure you can do it again if you push yourself a little harder. Maybe lay off those downers." Dave nodded at the bottle of shiny scarlet Vesparax capsules on the dresser by the whiskey bottle.

"And you should lay off that acid," Colin snapped at Dave.

Dave held his temper in control and tried again. "We've had a couple of hits, we've toured, we're beginning to take off..."

"Means nothing."

Dave's anger came over him full force. "Come off this pathetic routine!" he shouted. "Reaper is making money, but we need some new music. It's simple as that."

"Simple," Colin said flatly. He turned and glared at Dave. "I don't give a damn about our hit records, the tour, being on the road, the whiskey, the drugs, the girls. None of it."

They glared at each other.

"You've got a job to do, Colin," Dave said. "And that's to write lyrics. You wanted out of Clapham, and Reaper got us out of Clapham. Now it's time to take the next step..."

"I don't give a damn about Reaper taking the next step."

Dave felt his anger about to explode. He stepped out into the empty corridor, then back into the airless room. With a great effort, Dave lowered his voice. "Since we were in fourth form together, you always told me music is magic. Well, I believed you. Music—"

"Not this music." Colin slapped a pudgy hand down on his composition books. "Lyrics cribbed from the masters."

"So what?" Dave shouted at him. "I don't give a damn where you find the lyrics, just find them. I want Reaper to be famous. Can you understand that simple fact? I don't really care how we do it." Dave pointed at the poetry books on the dresser. "Copy out any bloody dead poet you like, just make it into lyrics that will make Reaper the top band in Britain."

Colin looked at the stack of books, then turned to the open window. "Reaper is never going to be great. I can't write original lyrics, and you can't write original melodies."

Dave came over and turned Colin around. "I'll find melodies. How I do it is my business. Yours is writing lyrics."

Colin twisted his shoulder out from under Dave's

hand. "Not anymore. Cribbing lyrics, playing in third-rate clubs—that's for Mick and Eric. What I want to do is write poetry. I can't play keyboards, not really. I know about a dozen chords, that's all. And I'm tired of them. I'm tired of all this crap." Colin shuffled his composition books into a neat stack and handed Dave the top one. "Here. Lyrics for your next ten tunes. You can steal ten tunes, I'm sure."

Dave took the book. "You're knotted up about me stealing a tune from some studio wog? That guy in the studio was on Alston's payroll. He gets paid by the hour, so he got paid for that tune."

Colin hauled a leather suitcase out from under the sagging bed and slammed his books into it, followed by clothes, the whiskey bottle, and his pills. "This is not my life." Dave stepped around him to the window and watched the summer breeze sway the trees above the stone wall. Behind him, he heard Colin close the suitcase, clomp down the stairs and out the front door. He watched him get in one of the vans and drive off.

A breeze lifted the thin cotton curtains then let them fall.

After a while, Dave went downstairs, grabbed his guitar, opened Colin's composition book to the first set of lyrics, turned on the tape recorder, and tried playing some of the music that had been in his head since the night before. His voice was not the best, but the music and the lyrics seemed to fit together. He sang it again, better this time. He played it back.

The archaic touch the words brought to the tunes was good. "Maybe add harpsichord. Or lute," he said to no one. He lit a cigarette. "These lyrics and these tunes can work. They will work."

He set aside his guitar and, leaving the front door open, walked down the sun-dappled lane to the pub. The sound of laughter shimmered out the door. Inside, Eric and Mick were holding forth to an audience of adoring local girls.

"Alright, guys," Dave interrupted. "Break's over. We've got some new music to work on."

There was silence. Then Eric put his pint on the bar. "Not just yet; we're still on break."

Nobody said anything. Mick drank the dregs of his pint and waved for another.

"And I said break's over," Dave growled.

Mick and Eric slid off their barstools. The girls backed away.

"Break's over when we say it is," Mick said. "You're not the dictator of the world."

"I'm the leader of the band!"

Mick and Eric exchanged glances. "Your band is shite. We should be back in London playing, not down here lying about—"

"Right," Dave shouted back. "Quit lying about and get back there and help me get this music down."

The was absolute silence in the pub for a long moment.

"I quit," Eric said.

"Me too," Mick added.

Eric tossed a wad of cash on the bar, and the two of them stalked out the door. The girls had disappeared. The bartender and the barmaid stood behind the bar, frowning in confusion.

Dave drew a deep breath. "No worries. They quit, and that's fine with me. I'll hire new players. I need to use your phone to make a trunk call to London."

The bartender pointed.

It only took Dave a few minutes to arrange with Alston to have four session men drive down from London next morning.

"Sorry about this," Dave told the bartender. "If there's still a balance due on their bill I'll pay it. Tell me tomorrow."

He sauntered down the lane, admiring the late-afternoon light on the dusty road, feeling better than he had in days, weeks. It would be good to have some fresh sidemen, play the new music, be done with Colin and Eric and Mick. When he walked through the stone arch and into the courtyard, he found it empty of vehicles. The second van was gone. "Good riddance!" he snorted.

As afternoon turned to evening, Dave played his two melodies over and over, each time getting them a little cleaner, a little sharper. After a while, he grabbed two beers and went down into the cool cellar where he paced, drank beer, paced, his temper high, but the music, the new music running through his head like liquid silver. Finally he slumped down in one of the velour chairs, and a deep silence settled. He thought he heard sounds, maybe distant laughter. But when he went upstairs, no one was there.

The generator had run out of fuel, so Dave lit a dozen candles, popped the last sliver of orange LSD into his mouth, and swallowed it. Then he took a tepid Brown's Bitter out of the inoperative fridge and made his way upstairs to his tiny bedroom, intending to write music. But evening had fallen, and with the darkening sky, he felt a vast exhaustion, so he lay down fully clothed. Sleep took him instantly.

He woke not knowing where he was. The room was stifling. Without the generator, the fan was no longer working. He opened the windows and latched them back. The moon was a sickle. The woods were a line of darkness above the grey stone wall, and the arched gateway to the paddock was entirely black. There was no wind, but a sense of faraway storms was in the night air. He saw a flicker that might have been lightning on the eastern horizon. Venus was a brilliant spark in the west.

He lay back down and let the acid take him into dreams half waking, half sleeping. People stood before him in the darkness beside the open window. His mother and father, sullen and stooped with drudgery, inarticulate as always. The bleak winter light on the brick streets of Clapham. The bully boys chasing him and Colin, throwing stones and taunting. Colin crying, running, his book bag flapping against the backs of his knees. The TransAt record shop, the scent so clear he felt himself reaching to touch the worn cardboard album covers.

Sounds impinged on Dave's ears in the darkness. He closed his eyes, but fluorescent rainbows were so intense he couldn't keep his eyes closed. The steady red beacon of Mars in the night sky now seemed comforting. He began to identify the tiny sounds around him. The sound of insects outside, the creak of cooling metal and stone. The ancient manse was speaking to him, and the sounds took on a rhythm and flowing melody, and behind it, at the edge of audibility, was a reedy piping.

"The wind," he said, thick-tongued. He rose from the dirty bed and went to the window. The sky was clear, Venus had set, and the sky belonged to the red glow of Mars.

Dave lay back down, but sleep was not within his reach. He listened to the sounds of the house and began to hear another sound amongst them— rhythmic clicking at the pace of footsteps. It was not the sound of footsteps on wood or carpet, but on stone. Something was walking in the wine cellar.

Dave went silently down the stairs to the great room, and amidst the tools found a hand torch the roadies had left. He switched it on and glanced around the room, but nothing moved. From the stairwell to the wine cellar he could hear the clicking of footsteps on the worn stone. Someone was down there. Probably a roadie.

Dave moved toward the head of the stone stairs down, but dread grew inside him, and he stopped and shrank back into a shadowed alcove at the head of the stair. There was a faint glow from below. He'd left lit candles burning on the tray—perhaps one or two still burned.

He clicked off the torch and listened to the steady clicking of footsteps. Sharp, slow clicking. Not shoes—hooves.

The clicking stopped as Dave huddled in the shadow, heart pounding. Then something began to slowly ascend the stone steps. Dave turned and ran, flung open the oak front door, ran across the lawn, through the gate, all the way across the sward to the edge of the woods.

There he stopped, gasping for air. There was no wind. Mars glowed above the ragged stone towers of Farley Manse. *If something comes through that gate,* Dave thought, *I'll click the torch on, throw it down, and leave it, while I run through the woods to the lane. Whatever it is will go after the torch, not after me.*

He woke thrashing the bedcovers. Out the open window, centered like a bull's-eye, was the baleful glow of Mars. "A dream," he muttered.

He lay back and closed his eyes. There seemed to be flickers of light, perhaps lightning from a distant thunderstorm, but when he got up and craned out the window, the night sky was clear. He thought he saw a human form move near the woods' edge. He heard a faraway piping. "Pan doesn't exist," he said aloud, his voice sounding strange in the tiny room. A melody flowed through his mind, endlessly evolving as it followed the piping. He felt an irrational panic freeze his body motionless.

It passed. The night became silent.

With shaking hands, Dave got a candle lit, then another. He sat down at the tiny table near the window, grabbed a composition book, and began scribbling music as fast as he could write. Fear dissipated; the music dominated his mind.

The sound of voices in the courtyard woke Dave from where he slumped at the table in his room. Outside, the sun was bright and straight overhead. In the courtyard, a van was discharging people. Guitar cases were handed out the back doors of the van. Dave leaned out the window and shouted, "Welcome to paradise! Come inside and get your gear set up."

Dave had one of the girls who had come with the musicians copy out five sets of music—Colin's lyrics over his own crazy scribbling from the night before. While she did so, the players—keyboard, bass, percussion, and another guitarist—set up and tuned their instruments.

The music was new and it was ragged, but all of them worked hard and without complaint. The keyboardist was fantastic. A sharp-faced kid with hair hanging over his eyes. He said almost nothing, but he could take the melody and move it all around to new places and back to the backbeat, and throughout it all call up the historic blood-deep melodies of ancient Britain built into Colin's lyrics. It was magic.

For Dave, it was a new and very pleasant experience working with the guys from London. They were seasoned musicians, knew how to add and subtract bits to fit his vision for a song. No arguments, but plenty of suggestions.

They had all decided to stay in rented rooms above the pub, so Dave had the manse to himself.

There were no clocks in the manse, but nobody cared if it was day or night. After sleeping, Dave would descend the ancient curved staircase with its missing bannister. There would be coffee, then he'd start picking out melodies. Eventually he and whoever else was around would eat something, then they would assemble and start working over the music. It was taking shape fast, and it was good. Strange but good.

The drugs had left his system, Dave realized.

When they had eight songs complete, and two almost complete, Dave called a break. Before they drifted outside to stretch their legs, smoke cigarettes, or whatever, Dave told them, "Thanks, guys. You're doing a great job. This stuff I've written is not even music, but you guys are turning it into music. I very much appreciate your work."

They acknowledged his thanks and went outside to stretch their legs.

Dave stood, lit a Players, and started for the wine cellar, realizing that was the first time he had ever thanked anyone playing music with him. He passed through the old kitchen. The generator was back on. He grabbed two bottles of Brown's Bitter and went down to the silent wine cellar, where a dozen candles burned bright on two trays. He sat down on the least-broken chair.

The keyboardist came down the steps. "Sorry to intrude, but..."

"Come on down," Dave said. "Would you mind bringing another beer?"

The kid returned with two bottles. He took a long drink from his, stood and stared around the old wine cellar. "Lot of years on this place."

Dave chuckled. "Not laughing at you, mate, just thinking what an understatement that is," Dave told him.

"I wanted to say that the music you've written is amazing," the kid blurted out. "It's unique. Not rock, not fusion, not blues, not the old British traditional music, and at the same time, all of them."

Dave smiled. "Thanks. I wrote out this stuff in the middle of the night, after some really strange dreams. Dreams, hallucinations, visions." Dave put out his cigarette and lit another.

"It's only after you blokes turn my scribblings into music that I am beginning to see what it's about. And it's about me."

The kid pulled his long hair back from his face. "That's true for all composers."

"I wouldn't know," Dave said. "I never met one."

They both laughed.

"Where are you from?" Dave asked.

"Brixton."

"I grew up on Kyrle Road, Clapham. Which is about as close to nowhere as you can get. It's a bitter, hard life there. Ever since I was a kid, I've been filled with frustration, anger, and fear. Me mum and me dad were automata; the grind of trying to live in that bleak place killed everything good in them. They were alive, but already half dead."

The kid looked at the stone floor.

"Another thing about growing up there—I'll tell you why I'll probably never be able to write a good pop song is because I've never felt love in me life. Sex, sure, but love, no. I think that was burned out of me by Clapham."

The kid was very embarrassed and started to leave.

"No—stay, listen to the rest of my confession, then give me absolution. And I'd take another beer while you're working on your absolution."

The kid returned in a minute with a cold bottle.

Dave continued, "Here's another thing: I never cared for that old-time American blues that everyone else was all crazy about."

"No?" The kid looked comically shocked.

"Shocking, isn't it?" Dave grinned at him. "Don't tell anyone, but those old American ex-slaves singing their blues songs—to me that's just whining and crying. I never felt that way—I was angry. At Clapham, at life, which is probably driving the anger you hear in my music." He laughed. "But my angry songs never sold. The songs that sold, 'Stay with Me' and 'No Time for Us,' came from another place."

The kid shuffled his feet, ducked his head, pushed his hair back from his eyes. "Well...I'm going..."

Dave waved at him. "Sorry to bleed all over you, but I felt like confessing, and you were the nearest person. Am I absolved?"

The kid grinned and started up the steps.

Twenty years later.

Dave was shown Colin's body on the medic's stretcher. A police officer said, "Found him dead this morning." Dave stared at Colin's features and tried to call up sorrow, even memories, but he could not. It didn't seem to be him anymore. The medical techs draped a sheet over the body and maneuvered it out the door of Colin's tiny flat.

One of the coppers came to Dave and opened his notebook. "Yours was the only name we found amongst his papers," he stated, "so we called you. Know who his next of kin might be?"

Dave shook his head. "I haven't seen or talked to Colin in fifteen years."

The copper held up a yellow plastic bottle of Vesparax capsules. "How long had he been taking these?"

"I don't know. I haven't seen him in..."

"Had you ever seen him taking these?"

"Twenty years ago, when we knew each other, he took them, I think. Said he needed them to sleep."

The coppers withdrew to a corner and conferred with each other in low voices. Dave overheard one say, "MO's already called in his verdict of an overdose of Vesparax and alcohol, probable suicide. There's no sign of foul play. This bloke was smart. He knew not to take too many pills too fast, or he would throw them up. So he sat drinking, taking the pills at intervals until he went unconscious. Didn't lie down, for fear of choking on vomit, the way most of them do. He just let his heart stop nice and easy."

One policeman looked at Dave. "You can go now."

Dave turned away, slipped four of Colin's composition books under his jumper, and left the flat. "Just like old times," he said to himself once he was out on the street. "Like stealing records from the old record shop."

Back in his own grimy flat, Dave poured himself some Bushmills and began reading Colin's composition books. He was expecting poetry, but they were a diary of sorts—reminiscences of school days, Colin crying to himself that he was overweight and had no friends. There were lists of old tunes, mostly American rockabilly and Gaelic pub music. Then quotes from poets. John Clare and Thomas Campion mostly. And statements: *They used to call me pansy-ass at school. No one ever understood how much that hurt. I did not tell that to anyone my whole life, because there was no one to tell it to.*

Dave turned a page and found an account of the first time they had met. It was when they'd both chanced to skip out of Latin class on the same day. "The old record shop on Lisle Street," Dave muttered, and the scent of dust, worn cardboard record jackets, and vinyl rose up in his mind. "The magic of music."

It had been a Wednesday he remembered. He was sixteen, in his last term at school, and he had skipped Latin class to walk across the bridge to Chelsea. He turned left on Lisle Street and into the TransAt record shop. Inside it was cool and dim, while outside, barely visible through grimy windows, the world went about its business. By the light of dusty bulbs bare overhead, Dave lost himself in the endless bins of albums. He would flip them past one after the next, then on to another bin and another, flipping past record after record.

Dave remembered whispering to Colin, "I'm nicking this record."

Colin looked aghast. He eyed the old man at the cash register.

"Go buy a record," Dave told Colin. "And while the old man's talking to you, I'll slip by." The plan worked perfectly.

"Here's to you, Colin." Dave raised his glass. "You were always too docile. You failed at writing music, you failed at writing poetry." Dave sipped and coughed. "Not that I've done any better. I wanted to be a rock star, but I couldn't write music either. Except for that one week at Farley Manse."

He flipped through the last pages of Colin's composition books, the entries becoming fewer and shorter.

Ridiculous, despite all my effort, all my pretensions. In the end, I fall back on Keats: "Was it a vision, or a waking dream? Fled is that music: Do I wake or sleep?" I think of Farley Manse, a dryad dying, ethereal words drifting up to a cloudless sky.

None of it matters.

Dave poured himself more whiskey and said in a voice coarse from a quarter of a million cigarettes,

"You're right, Colin. None of it matters. Here's to you Colin, and me and Reaper, failures all." He took a sip from his glass and savored the fire on his tongue.

Dave coughed a laugh. "I still remember the look on Alston's face when I played him the tracks of *Dryad's Dream*. 'Uncommercial crap!' he screamed. Then he billed me for the cost of the entire stay at Farley. I had to sell him the rights to the name Reaper, and the rights to all our music, to cover the cost. After that I was just his employee, a contract slave. I went on endless tours as lead singer for a bunch of hired musicians playing under the name Reaper. I was drunk all day, every day, for all those years." Dave poured himself the last of the whiskey. "Now the doctors tell me I've only got a few months to live. Liver cancer and lung cancer." He held up his glass of amber whiskey and his cigarette. "Alcohol and tobacco—the only ones who did stay with me."

For a time, Dave sat staring straight ahead, lost in a haze of painkillers. Then he resumed muttering. "All those years on the road, playing crap music. Wasted. My whole life wasted. All but those few days in the spring of 1973, when I felt the magic. The magic that you and I used to talk about, Colin. For a few moments suspended outside of time, I could play the music of dreams and illusions."

A bout of coughing stopped Dave's mutter. When it ended, he took a drag on his cigarette. "I heard Alston sold the rights to *Dryad's Dream* to Island Records for next to nothing. They pressed a few copies, but then the master tapes got lost."

Dave's head drooped forward as alcohol and painkillers slowed him. He watched cigarette smoke rise and ripple, and for a moment sensed shadowy forms and distant mocking laughter. "Music is invisible—doesn't exist. And it doesn't matter anyway. None of it does."

In Chelsea, the block where TransAt record shop once stood is now a glass and steel office monolith. Clapham has gentrified; the brick row houses of Kyrle Road have been gutted and refurbished to glossy splendor. In the deep woods of Wiltshire, Farley Manse has become a ruin—its roof fallen in, its furniture, carpets, pennants, and paintings rotting away to nothing.

A band called Reaper still appears in London clubs playing commercial music from the 1970s. None of the ever-changing lineup of hired musicians know anything of Dave or Colin or Farley Manse. But original copies of *Dryad's Dream* are now collector's items.

THE SCENT OF SANDALWOOD

It was a mild October afternoon in 1970 when a girl driving a white Olds Cutlass wheeled into the gas station. I put down my SF paperback and went out to the pumps, hoping to find some gorgeous babe. But the girl who got out of the car was not a gorgeous blonde. This girl had an ordinary body, ordinary long brown hair in a ponytail, and, I was pretty sure, an ordinary face behind her sunglasses. "Fill her up," she told me and went off in the direction of the rest rooms.

I had the tank full and the bugs cleaned off her windshield by the time she returned. "Twenty gallons," I told her. "$6.60." It was three o'clock—closing time on Saturday—and I was eager to close up and go eat a late lunch. I took her money, thanked her, and went into the office to put the cash in the safe and lock up.

When I came back out she was still there, leaning against her car, squinting at the Heidelberg restaurant sign. The October afternoon was bright and cool—perfect autumn weather.

"I'm trying to decide if I ought to eat something now, then drive straight through to Bloomington," she told me. "Or start driving now and stop to eat somewhere farther along. Food any good in that place?" She nodded toward the Heidelberg.

"Yeah, pretty good," I told her. "I'm going there now. Want to join me?" I guess in the back of my mind I began to build a fantasy that she and I would spend the afternoon drinking beer, then she would spend the night with me. All twenty-one-year-old guys have these fantasies. But since I'd just received my draft notice, these serendipitous sex fantasies had taken on new urgency. Live for today suddenly seemed like a really good idea.

"Yeah." She nodded and tossed her sunglasses on the dash. "I'm hungry now, and eating here will postpone my having to get back in the car for another thirty minutes."

We found a booth about halfway back. With her glasses off, I saw she had some pimple scars on her face that didn't help her ordinary looks, but when she smiled, she looked good. Besides, I'd already learned that women's looks weren't that important, unless you had a trophy date and were trying to impress the other guys. Then appearance was critical.

We both ordered Heidelberg Specials—breaded and fried veal tenderloins with fries and dill pickle slices. I ordered a draft beer, which in the Heidelberg meant Hamm's. She ordered a Coke.

"Where are you coming from? Or going to?" I said, just to get some conversation going.

"Coming from San Francisco," she said. "Going to Bloomington, Indiana."

Our food came, and we ate in silence. Afterward, she lit a Kool, and we sat, me savoring my beer, her staring at the wall opposite. Apparently she had a lot on her mind, or else my scintillating conversation was falling short of her expectations. Like I said, she didn't look that good, but she had a special magnetism that some girls have regardless of plain looks. She seemed to have some inner fire, and maybe a bit of inner anger.

I finished my beer and decided to have a second one. "I know you're driving, but one beer won't hurt," I told her. "I'm buying."

She waved her hand. "Had to give up drinking. I was drinking way too much. There is such a thing as an addictive personality, you know."

That surprised me. I guessed she was only a couple of years older than me. But I didn't want to pry into her drinking problem. That's definitely not the way to get a girl into bed.

"Alcohol is hard enough to stop," she told me. "But the hard drugs, and the...lifestyle of the rockers in San Francisco would be just about impossible to stop. At least for me it would."

She ground out her cigarette and squinted at my left shirt pocket. I still had on one of the Standard

Oil gas station shirts. "Chris, is it?" she said. "I'm just winding down from a lot of driving, so I'm probably babbling, or staring at the wall. Sorry." Then she added, "I've been in San Francisco all summer on field research. I'm in sociology, doing my thesis on the rock music scene there."

"San Francisco," I breathed. "Wow. Haight-Ashbury, flower power, and all that music: Quicksilver, Airplane, Big Brother, Dead...did you talk to those guys, interview them?"

"Yeah," she said without enthusiasm. "I've seen them up close." She went back to staring at the wall.

I decided to change the subject. "By the way, my name's not Chris." I pointed at the name badge sewn onto my shirt. "When I come to work, I just put on whatever clean shirt is hanging in the closet in the gas station. Some days I'm Chris, some days I'm Allen." I grinned. "It's fun changing your identity."

She gave me a deep look, then smiled. "You are right about that. Definitely right that changing your identity is sometimes a good thing."

"Sounds like you've—"

"I'll tell you this," she cut me off. "Lots of those big rock stars ought to change their personalities. They get to the point where their stage persona becomes them; they become their stage persona. And everybody expects that stage persona to take endless drugs, live a chaotic lifestyle, have sex with anybody anytime, all that." She lit another cigarette. "Why am I telling you this?" She sometimes had a kind of coarseness about her, a way of asking questions a little too directly, that put me off.

"I'll tell you why," I said, deciding to be more direct myself. "Because lots of times, we find it easier to tell things to strangers than to our friends, or girlfriends, or boyfriends. You have a boyfriend in Bloomington?"

She laughed at that. "Don't get angry, Chris. I've spent all summer interviewing 'stars' who won't listen to you unless you really get pushy with them. They are always stoned, and in any case, they think somebody like me, some nobody college girl, is not worth talking to." She put her hand on my arm. "So I learned to get a little pushy. Don't get uptight." She gave me a smile that I really liked.

"My real name is Mark," I told her with a smile, "but you can call me Chris or Allen or anything you like."

"I think I like Chris," she told me. "About my boyfriend—yes, I do have a 'significant other,' as I'd prefer to call it."

"Not to get too pushy," I said, "but that's a rather cold term, isn't it? Significant other?"

She shrugged. "We like it. We're both rather independent people. We like being together, but we like time alone too. He's got his career and I've got mine." She gave me a hard look. "But I don't play around, and neither does he. Too many people want it both ways: a steady relationship, and new partners every night. That doesn't work. Half the big stars I interviewed were having sex with every groupie that threw herself at him, and at the same time whining about how lonely they were because they couldn't find a real relationship. What hogwash."

"Hogwash." I smiled. "You must be from the Midwest, like me."

"Texas," she told me. "I've only been in Indiana a year. I'm in the master's program at IU. But I like it there. I'll probably stay and get a PhD."

"You girls are lucky," I told her. "I'd love to go to grad school. But I can't. I've already gotten my draft notice."

She touched my hand. "Sorry."

I ordered another beer. "I don't like it. But I have learned to accept it. Knowing I have to go into the army, knowing I'll probably go to Vietnam, and not knowing what will happen over there, has given me a whole new perspective. I value the small things a lot more now. I wish I did have a steady relationship though. Dating around is overrated." I drank some beer. "Sorry to get so philosophical."

"No need to say you're sorry." She leaned forward, elbows on the table. "Because what you just said is exactly what I learned this summer in San Francisco. In fact, that's going to be the central point of my thesis, I think—valuing the small things in life. Something like that." She leaned back in the booth and took a long drag on her cigarette. "At the same time, we have to kind of balance that acceptance with a reasonable ambition, and our determination to make something of ourselves. And do it without regret."

"You can't be two people at once." I smiled. "Except in the parallel timeline stories I read."

She ignored my smile. "I'll tell you about regret. A few years ago, I wanted to be a singer. Really wanted it. And tried hard to be one, but couldn't make a go of it. It's taken me nearly six years to get that regret out of my mind. To accept that I will never be a famous singer. When I die, nobody will know my name." She gave me a very direct look. "This summer in San Francisco brought that regret back for a while. I started wondering if I'd quit trying too soon. Especially when I interviewed Grace Slick. She made it, and made it big. I had to work hard to keep from thinking, 'Maybe I ought to try again. Maybe it's not too late for me.' But I also could see that she stayed away from the really self-destructive stuff— drugs and lifestyle and all that. She has a life separate from being a singer. I think if I had become famous, my addictive personality would have gotten me killed fairly soon."

Her frown drove me to try to change the subject. "Three years ago, my buddies and me drove to San Francisco for a couple of weeks. It was great. I'm a science fiction and fantasy reader, and Haight-Ashbury was a fantasy world. People living new lifestyles, exploring all sensations...I thought about dropping out and staying there...I would have gotten really caught up in all that if I'd stayed. Maybe not a good thing."

"Definitely not a good thing. Things have changed since you were there," she said in a bitter tone. "A few years ago, Haight-Ashbury may have been the center of the universe, but now the old hippie days are gone. Now it's money and drugs, mostly drugs. There's a lot of bad vibes." She was frowning as she looked at her watch for the fourth time. "Anyway, I've got to get going."

I put my hand on her forearm. "Stay until I finish this beer; five more minutes. Tell me something brighter. Tell me about a parallel timeline. The one where the bright world we all imagined when the counterculture took over the world became reality." I hid my face behind my beer glass. "Sorry. Read as much science fiction as I do, and pretty soon you start believing parallel timelines might really exist."

She eased back in the booth. "Well now that you mention alternate timelines, let me tell you a story. I'll spend five more minutes, then I'm on my way, OK?"

"I love stories." I grinned. "But before you do, you mentioned you'd interviewed Grace Slick. Did you interview the lead singer for Big Brother? I can't think of her name right now. She and Slick are clearly the top two singers in all of rock. What's her name and what's she like?"

"Kathi McDonald. I did interview her, and yes, she is both a great singer and a great person. Someone who can balance being a star with having a real life. She was polite, interesting—I envy her a lot." She started staring at the wall again, remembering.

"Now tell me your story," I prompted.

"OK. Promise not to laugh. This just happened last night, and I haven't been able to get it out of my mind all day today. If there really are parallel timelines, I was in one."

"Sounds good to me," I told her.

"It wasn't," she said and lit another cigarette. "After driving all day yesterday, I checked into a motel somewhere in eastern Colorado. Went straight to bed and right to sleep. I was exhausted. But just before dawn, I woke up. Didn't know where I was. All motel rooms kind of look the same, you know?" She examined the end of her cigarette. "It was very strange. I was still half asleep, but somehow I had the feeling that I wasn't in the same motel room. But here's the real shocker: I started to get out of bed, thought I'd get dressed and start driving since I was already awake, but as I started to swing my feet out of bed, I look down beside the bed, and there's someone lying there."

"Wow!" I gasped.

"A girl, about my age; she wasn't moving at all. She was dressed in flashy clothes, like the rockers I'd been seeing in San Francisco all summer. Scared the hell out of me. I just froze. I couldn't even move to call the front desk, the cops, anybody. But here's an even bigger shocker: she was lying on her back, and in the dawn light coming in around the drapes, I could see that she was me."

I downed the last of my beer. "That is one hell of a dream. So what did you do?"

"I got out of bed on the other side, came around, and tried to help her up, but she was dead, her body already cool. A syringe and tie and some white powder were right there on the carpet beside her. She'd apparently OD'd. I went over and sat in the chair, my mind in a whirl. After a minute, I realized I was smelling the scent of sandalwood. I know that scent, since I sometimes wear it myself. Anyway, I went back around the bed, thinking I'd try to get her body up on the bed, then call the front desk, and guess what? She was not there. No body, no drugs, just bare carpet. A dream I guess." She stubbed out her cigarette. "But I'll tell you this—I have never had a dream that was as real as that one."

I left some cash on the table and walked her out to her car. The afternoon was that perfect soft autumn when the light and the air temperature are both perfect.

"You'd make a pretty good field sociologist," she told me. "You know how to listen. Even to crazy dreams."

I grinned. "And you'd make a pretty good science fiction writer."

"That dream felt as real as all this feels now," she said, waving her hand around at the street, the buildings, the fine October sunshine. "I knew without a doubt that that dead girl was me. Another me, maybe a me from one of your parallel timelines. If I believed in the occult, which I don't, I'd think maybe that other me had been crying out to me across the timelines, trying to get help." She paused, then shook her head. "That's what *National Enquirer* would probably report. But one thing that dream has done is erase the last little bit of regret I had that I will never be a rock star."

"And that nobody will ever know your name," I added. "Except your SO, your friends, your family, your colleagues—a lot of people. You'll be just like all the rest of us." I laughed. "Do me a favor. When your thesis is finished, send me a copy. I'd like to read it, even if your dream is not in it."

She laughed too. "Read my thesis? Nobody reads master's degree theses, not even the examining committee. They just check to see if the endnotes and chapter heads are formatted right. But give me your address, and I'll mail you one when it's done."

I wrote my name and address on a scrap of paper and handed it to her. She frowned. "Not much of an address: Care of US Army?"

"I've heard the army's pretty good at getting mail to the troops. Not much good at anything else, but they get the mail to you. At least that's what my buddies tell me."

She gave me a hug and a kiss on the cheek before she got in her car. "Thanks for listening to my crazy dream, and thanks for lunch." She started the car and put it in gear.

"Speaking of nobody ever knowing your name," I said. "What is your name?"

As she pulled away, she waved and called back to me, "Janis—Janis Joplin."

California Dreaming

I showed up at Western Recording Studios at nine in the morning, same as always. Same old cubbyhole I'd been assigned when I came to work for MGT Records ten years ago. As soon as I sat down, Don Jasper, MGT's Production Manager—whom I hated—walked in with his usual cigar clenched in his teeth. He laid a legal form on my desk.

"JR, I'll make this easy for you to understand: this is an extension of your contract for five more years. You are on exclusive contract to MGT, paid weekly, no royalties for performing, recording, or publishing; your name's not going to be on any recording; and you're not going on tour as sideman for anybody. Got it?"

I didn't bother looking at the paper. "Well, that's not what I want." I looked Jasper in the eye and saw his slow burn starting. "I want 2 percent royalty on every record this company sells of any song I wrote or recorded or both."

Jasper removed the cigar from his mouth. "JR, you don't seem to understand." He sounded like a father talking to a retarded child. "I *own* you. If you want to make music in LA, you'll do it for MGT Records on these terms. If you don't sign that paper right now, you'd better collect your stuff, vacate this office, and start driving in a straight line out of this town." He spat into the corner.

One of the hulking morons Jasper kept on payroll as "security guards" appeared in the doorway.

"If you don't work for me, you won't work for anybody in this town or anywhere else." He put the cigar back in his mouth and turned to leave, but paused in the doorway. "My boys won't break up your fingers. You'll need them to make music for me, but they may rearrange your face a little."

The guard stood there, impassive. I looked at the paper on my desk for a moment, then got out a pen, scrawled across the signature line, and handed it to the gorilla. Without looking at it he departed. I knew I had about five minutes to be gone from the building, since I'd written "Screw you, Jasper" on the signature line.

I grabbed my acoustic guitar and scuttled out the door. In the hallway I paused, went back inside, got the master tape from yesterday's recording session, and put it in my pocket. MGT was already advertising the release of The Dragsters next album, and I had the only tape of it in my pocket. I laughed, hopped in my 'Vette, and wound through traffic to Manhattan Beach. I felt full of high spirits, like a kid cutting class.

And I'd tweaked Jasper's nose by stealing his music.

"My music," I corrected myself. "He'll beg me to bring it back, then we can talk about a new contract for me." Talking aloud, I didn't notice the maroon Buick a few car lengths behind me keeping a careful distance.

At Manhattan Pier it was sunny; the smog was inland. A few tourists strolling the Pier, a dozen surfers out at the break, a few couples here and there.

Walking along the cold sand, watching others enjoying the beach, I began to feel the way I always did when I came to the beach.

Lonely.

"Alone on the Beach" had been one of my best-selling songs. I'd written it four years ago, but the emptiness in my heart hadn't changed in four years. There was nobody I cared about, and nobody cared about me.

I got back in my 'Vette and drove east, going no-where, trying not to think about my future. Eventually I found myself northbound on the I-395. I had about sixty dollars in my billfold and nothing in the bank. *And* I knew Jasper had not been kidding when he told me that if I quit working for him, I'd never work for any recording studio again. Jasper, the Heinrich Himmler of the LA music industry.

My mind elsewhere, I still did not notice the maroon Buick following me as the freeway wound north through the desert. Past China Lake Navy Station the freeway began to climb the eastern slope of the Sierras. The sun was already behind the mountains, and I was beginning to realize I was exhausted, hungry, and had no place to stay for the night. Or any future nights.

Past Owens Lake I stopped to get gas at a Quick-Stop. The air was cool and sweet with the scent of pine.

"How far to the next town?" I asked the guy behind the counter.

"Twenty miles to Crystal Village, which you can barely call a town. Bishop's the next real town. It's about an hour's drive north. Nice car you've got there."

"Yeah, thanks." I took my Coke and bag of Doritos and got back in my 'Vette and headed north, but I could tell I was too tired to make it to Bishop. I forced myself to keep going. Soon a constellation of lights turned themselves into an exit, a gas station, and a gold rush era house that had been refurbished as a B&B. A rustic wooden sign said "Crystal Village." I pulled up in front of the B&B.

The front door was heavy oak with a big glass oval decorated with etched flowers. A little bell tinkled as I entered. Behind the counter a slim girl was rolling light blue paint onto a wall of newly installed sheetrock. She was dressed in the standard Sierras uniform of blue jeans and plaid shirt, nondescript brown hair pulled back in a ponytail.

"We're closed for remodeling," she said without looking around. "Nearest motel's up in Bishop."

I stood where I was. After a moment she set the paint roller in its tray and stepped around the counter. She was short, maybe 5'2", and wouldn't have been bad looking except for the scowl on her face.

"Look," she said. "We're not open, OK?"

I continued to stand there.

"You running away from somebody? The police, for example?"

"No . . ." I said, not sounding very convincing. "Do I look like a fugitive?"

"Yes."

We continued to stand there, facing each other like some western movie showdown on main street. Finally, she rolled her eyes and said, "Against my better judgment, I'll rent you the one room we've got finished. Roger keeps telling me I need get some revenue coming anyway. And besides, if you try to keep driving in the condition you're in, you'll run off the road and I'll have that on my conscience."

"Thanks," I told her, with a smile she didn't return. "You're right, I'm dead tired. I've been driving since—"

"Go get your luggage."

I hauled my guitar case and backpack into the lobby. "Place looks nice," I said; exhaustion had settled on me like a lead weight.

"It will when we get it finished. That'll be eighty dollars," she said matter-of-factly. With her no-nonsense expression I figured she was pretty much a matter-of-fact kind of person all around. I opened my billfold and pulled out all my cash, sixty dollars.

She deftly extracted two of them and put them in the old-fashioned cash register.

"I'll give it to you for forty dollars, tonight only. Leave your car where it is. Your room's right around the corner here, by the staircase."

The room decor matched the exterior of the building, imitation Nob Hill, gingerbread-studded 1890s splendor, including a big four-poster bed. She put fresh towels in the bathroom and ran some water in the sink.

"Good. The new hot water heater is working," she pronounced. "I need you out of here first thing in the morning."

I guess my irritation showed. She softened her tone. "I mean, I've got a lot of work to get done on this place tomorrow and need to start early, so . . ."

"I'll be out of here early."

She glanced at my guitar case. "You a musician?"

I wanted only to lie down on that big, inviting bed and forget today. "Not anymore."

"Here's the room key." She laid a metal key hanging

from a large oval plastic tag on a doily-covered table and stepped out into the foyer. "And stay out of the upstairs." She waved a hand at a staircase that disappeared up into darkness. "There are boards, sheet rock, nails, exposed wires . . ."

"I'm going straight to bed," I told her and closed the door.

Strange knocking sounds woke me. The clock said twelve thirty. I sat up on fragrant sheets, disoriented by the four-poster bed I was in. Then I got up, pulled on my clothes, and looked around for a flashlight, but could find nothing. I turned on the room lights and looked out in the foyer. Nobody there.

A man's voice floated down from the darkened stairs. "Somebody here? Sorry to wake you. I'm a carpenter helping with the remodel."

"In the middle of the night?"

He came downstairs into the light—a mild looking guy, maybe forty-five years old, looking like everybody else in the Sierras: pony tail, worn jeans, plaid shirt, work boots, weathered face.

"Yeah," he said. "Middle of the night. I'm helping Arabella. I live right next door, so I come over here whenever I have some time." He grinned. "Sometimes I like it better working when she's not around. She's kinda bossy. But she thinks she's got to be independent. Guess I talk too much." He grinned again. "My name's Roger."

"I'm JR."

"I can skip working tonight," he said while unabashedly peering into my room. "I see you're a guitarist. What do you play?"

"I used to play surf rock. Back in LA."

"I used to love surf rock. When I lived in LA." He nodded. "Hey, drink a beer with me and play me some tunes. I live right next door. I like drinking beer and talking about music, but this town closes up at nine . . ."

I started to tell him that I didn't have time to sit around in the middle of the night drinking beer with some old Sierra hippie. Then I started thinking, *What's my hurry? I'm not going anywhere in particular. I told— was her name Arabella?—that I'd be gone first thing in the morning, and I planned to, but I'd slept soundly, I felt rested, and a beer or two sounded pretty good.*

"Why not?" I said.

"That's the Sierra spirit," he said softly. "Follow me and stay close." He clicked on his flashlight and I followed him up the stairs. "Got sheetrock leaning against the wall in the hallway."

"You live next door?"

"Yeah." He opened a door onto a wooden second-story catwalk that connected the back of the B&B to another building. "Way back when Arabella's parents bought both these buildings, they were a residence with a connected radio station. This building," he whispered, opened a creaking wooden door, "was the radio station on the second floor with parking on the lower level. The previous owners put in a connecting walkway between the two buildings. My wife, Annie and I—she's upstairs sleeping so be a little quiet— rent the old radio station from Arabella and live in it. It's got a small but nice bedroom, bath, and kitchen. And our rent payments give Arabella a bit of extra income."

Inside was a room with a worn, red Indian carpet on the floor, a sagging wooden couch in faux cowboy style, and a couple of comfortable looking armchairs. There was a wall of vinyl records on one side of the room and a booth with two turntables, microphones, headsets, and all the usual radio station stuff on the other side. The glass had been removed from the booth.

I was smiling. "Love the smell of a studio," I told him. He handed me a can of beer, some brand I'd never heard of, and we sank into the chairs.

"How long's this station been off the air?"

"Probably twenty years. Long before Annie and I got here. Arabella told me it shut down about the time her parents bought these two buildings."

"Must be fun looking through all the old vinyl," I said. The beer tasted great.

"Yeah, it has been. Most of these old records were here when we moved in; some of them we brought with us from LA. That's about all we brought, the clothes on our backs and my record collection."

"Got your priorities straight," I told him.

"Turntables still work," he said, indicating the equipment in the control booth. "And the monitoring amps and speakers work, so sometimes I play records and pretend I'm on the air again. I used to be a DJ." He drank long from his beer. "But that was another lifetime."

I set my empty beer can on the floor and he handed me another.

"What do you do in this lifetime, except help Arabella remodel?"

"I'm the maintenance man at Harris Lumber down in Newton. It's about ten miles east of here."

"Maintenance man by day, remodeler by night, and phantom DJ in between." I raised my beer can in a toast. "Sounds like the Sierras."

"I like it." He went up to sit in the DJ booth. The speakers came on with a subdued pop. "Got to keep it low, Annie's sleeping." He put a 45 on one of the turntables and said into the microphone in a gentle voice that sounded very familiar, "This is 93 KHJ, surf radio in Los Angeles. Here's a song everybody will remember." The song was "Surfer Girl" by the Beach Boys.

While it played softly, he came down out of the booth and sat in his chair. "I like being a ghost DJ, playing the old tunes just for myself and Annie and Arabella. I could have stayed in LA, but it was driving me crazy. I was always angry, at the station manager, at the record distributors, at the advertisers, everybody."

"So you quit."

"Yeah." He opened another can of beer for himself. "March 1968. I was at KFWB by then. The owners of the station decided to change format, to save money, so it became a talk radio station. I quit at the end of my shift that day. Annie and I loaded the car, put the house in Canoga Park up for sale, and started driving north." He took a long slug of beer. "And here we are."

"When you did your radio voice just now ... I know I've heard you before, maybe we met somewhere. You're not the 'Real Don Steele' are you?"

"No, I'm not Don." He stared at the carpet. "I used to be Roger Jansen. And we have met before. In fact, you and I wrote a few songs together." He turned his head slightly and put on a Hollywood smile.

"Roger Jansen!" I said, laughing. "It's is good to see you. I often wondered where you'd gone. You and I wrote 'Kustom Kar Kutie' back in 1963, remember?"

He nodded. "Yeah, that was a fun day. And that song, our song ... who'd MGT put on the label ... the Daytona's or some such? Our song went to number ten on the Top 100." He sounded proud.

"That was back when DJ's could push a song into the Top Ten." I laughed long and loud, then clapped my hand over my mouth. "Sorry, I know your wife's trying to sleep. Roger Jansen. Man! How did you end up here?"

"Pure chance. We were driving north, just stopped here for the night. Been here ever since. The old B&B

was pretty run down at the time. Arabella's parents had just died and willed her this place. She'd moved up here and was trying to run it by herself."

"Why didn't she just sell it?"

"Sentiment. Her parents had moved up here from Hermosa Beach and had run it for ten years. She knows she could sell these buildings for a lot of money." He looked thoughtful. "But I believe she doesn't know what she'd do with herself if she did sell this place."

The record had ended. "I could play you another record," Roger said, "but I'd rather hear you play." He glanced at my guitar case.

So I got out my guitar. "You'll remember this one," I told him and played the first six bars of a hit tune from 1967, stopping at the suspended chord which comes just before the group starts singing.

A smile broke over his face. "Love that song. You wrote it?"

"No, but I composed and played that part on their record. John and Michelle wrote the melody and the lyrics. They were rehearsing at Western Studios where I worked. At that time they were kind of folkies, not real electric, you know? Their version just had them start in singing the words. I suggested the guitar lead-in which made it less folksy and more rock." I realized I was babbling and took a long shot of beer to shut myself up.

"Your lead-in made that song famous. Congratulations," Roger told me, raising his beer in salute.

"Yeah, it made the song famous, but it didn't make me famous."

Roger settled back while I ran through my tale of woe. I kept my fingers moving softly over the strings as I explained just how evil the music business was, while at the same time how beautiful the music itself was. He offered me a beer, which I refused. "But I love making music. I may go back to LA . . ."

He shrugged. "You sure you want to go back to work for the jerks you just described?"

"What else can I do? I love making music, and they control the music business."

"You sound like Arabella. Like there's only one option in life."

"Despite the jerks at MGT," I told him. "When I was first working there in the early sixties, when you and I and all those other guys were writing and singing that music, those were some of the best days of my life . . ."

"You just told me the opposite. You said you always felt like an outsider; you were always alone . . . alone on the beach. Wasn't that one of your songs?"

"Yeah, it was. But LA was perfect in those days, and my music was part of that perfection."

"I used to tell Annie the same thing," he said. "Right after complaining about how unhappy I was."

"What did she tell you?"

"Quit complaining, figure out what you really want, then do it. I always thought I wanted to be a big record producer. But I'm a heck of lot happier as a handyman here than I was as a semi-famous DJ back in LA. If I'd stayed there, I probably would have turned into one of those jerks you just described." He finished his third beer. "Besides, were the good old days really so good?"

I opened my mouth to rebut his statement, then closed it. Thinking back, it all seemed great, but I tended not to remember all the loneliness I used to feel. *I never really wanted the surfing scene—parties all the time, two girls for every guy . . . all that stuff Jan and Dean used to sing about. What I really wanted was a steady girlfriend and to be able to write and play music that people liked. I never wanted to be a big star.*

Roger was peering out the window that overlooked the roof of the B&B.

"That's strange."

"What's strange?" I said closing the little fridge. "That I changed my mind about having another beer?"

"There's a car parked across the street, lights off, but people in it. It wasn't there an hour ago. And it's nobody from around here. I know everybody's car."

There were footsteps on the catwalk outside. Arabella came in. "I heard voices, and music." I got out another beer and handed it to her. She seated herself on the ancient sofa. "You're a pretty good guitarist, or was that a record?"

I played the opening bars of the same Mamas and Papas song.

"Why'd you choose that one?" Arabella asked. "It's a sad song . . . brown leaves and gray skies."

"You know anything about that car across the street?" Roger interrupted.

"I didn't notice one," she said.

I'd had two beers, was feeling pretty mellow, and was about to give Arabella the long, sad story of my life, but fortunately Roger interrupted.

"JR and I were just talking about the old days, back in LA."

Arabella rolled her eyes. "The good old days."

Roger smiled indulgently. "No need to act so superior; you've told me a dozen times how much fun it is listening to these old records. They were part of our lives growing up."

I saw the side of her neck color slightly as she blushed.

"When you actually listen to those oldies," Arabella said, "they are pretty crappy."

"But they're full of nostalgia," Roger said. "JR, and me, and the musicians, the bands, the singers, the one-hit-wonders who had a song on the radio for a few weeks then disappeared forever. We're all ghosts now."

I nodded. "Especially the session men, like me, who made the music but didn't get their name on the song." I set my guitar aside. "Not much of a legacy we're leaving is it, Roger?"

He was rummaging around in cabinets. "Got to be a reserve six-pack here somewhere." He found one and put it in the fridge. "I disagree. I think we are leaving a pretty nice legacy." He opened a warm beer and drank some.

"People listen to the old songs and it brings a smile to their face." Roger continued. "They're remembering the good times they had when those songs were on the radio. And that's not a bad legacy for you and me to leave. Happiness."

I nodded slowly.

Roger laughed. "Forget about the jerks who run the record companies. What matters is the music." He took a drink of his beer.

"Roger tells me you grew up in LA too," I said to Arabella. She looked a lot better when she smiled.

"Hermosa Beach."

"Dewey Weber and Greg Knoll both had surf shops there."

"I know. You a surfer?"

"No, but I used to write a lot of surf music. I visited their shops a time or two just to get a feel for the whole surfing scene."

"But you're leaving all that behind, right?"

"Maybe," I said, strumming a couple of chords on my guitar. "I don't think I've completely decided yet. I know a way to get my old job back at MGT Records."

Arabella shook her head. "Wasn't there a song

about not being able to make up your mind?"

"'Lovin' Spoonful,'" I told her.

A crash sounded downstairs in the B&B. Roger and Arabella jumped to their feet.

"What was that?" Roger said.

"I'm going to go find out," Arabella said and scurried out onto the catwalk between buildings.

"Not by yourself you're not," Roger said following her out. I put down my guitar, crossed the catwalk, and crept into the dark corridor clogged with construction material. There was the sound of a scuffle downstairs, then a man said, "Go find him."

I turned to go, but a flashlight beam from downstairs picked me out. "Hey, you! Get down here," a guy shouted at me.

In the foyer there were three men wearing slacks and sports jackets. One had a hat on—the kind of hat you'd see at Dino's on Sunset Strip.

One of the intruders had Arabella in a hammerlock. Roger was face down on the floor, a thug holding him down with one knee.

"Ah," the man in the hat grunted. "Our little runaway. Didn't you sing that song Mr. Hotshot Rock and Roll Star?"

"Del Shannon sang it," I said.

"Like I care? You've got something that don't belong to you. Give it to me or she's going to get her face rearranged." The thug holding Arabella waved a razor knife around her face.

"I've got money," Roger said into the carpet. The thugs ignored him. Hat-man got right up in my face.

"Make this easy for all of us, JR. Give me the tape you stole from MGT Records."

I rushed into my room, dug through my backpack, and got the cassette tape.

"Now play it," hat-man said, "just to make sure you're handing us the right tape." His carnivorous smile widened. "First song should be 'Everywhere You Go.'"

"There's no cassette player here," Arabella said in a voice choked with fear.

"My car has one," I told them. We all trooped out into the cold night, the thugs half-dragging Roger and Arabella. I started my car and played a few minutes of the tape while they stood there breathing frost into the night air.

"OK," hat-man said. He held out his hand and I gave him the tape. He put his face up to mine and said in a quiet voice, "I ought to beat your face in just because you're stupid, but I won't. Not this time. But if I ever see you again, I will." He turned to the big thug who'd let go of Arabella.

"Help him get the message, Al." The big guy took a concrete block from the stack near the driveway and heaved it through the windshield of my 'Vette. Then the three of them strolled across the street, got in the maroon Buick, and drove off.

"Who were those guys?" Arabella breathed. We went into the foyer and closed the door. Arabella was shivering so I helped her to the sofa; Roger got a blanket from my bedroom and draped it around her. "I'm not used to being threatened," she said in a shaky voice. "I'm sorry."

"I'm the one who should be sorry," I told her. "Those guys were after me, not you. They were sent to get back a tape I took."

"Why'd you steal a tape?" Roger asked.

"I don't consider it stealing. It was a tape of music I wrote and me and some other session guys recorded. It was my music. But MGT records will sell it with a made-up band's name on the record, and MGT records keeps all the profits." I nodded toward the smashed windshield of my 'Vette. "That's my thank you from MGT records."

A bleary-eyed woman in jeans and sweatshirt eased down the stairs brandishing a big flashlight like a weapon.

"Annie," Roger said. He pulled her to him. "Everything's alright."

I felt a wave of jealousy. It was a relationship like Roger and Annie's that I'd wanted my whole life.

"Some guys broke in, looking for a tape JR had," Roger gestured toward me. "He gave it to them and they left."

Annie just shook her head. "And smashed out his car window too? All that for a tape?"

"Yeah," I told Annie. "But they won't be back," I hoped. "My former boss is not going to waste more time and money tormenting me. He'll hire some other session-man to make music for him and he'll forget about me. Oh, if he catches me recording for some other company, things could get tight. But he won't. I'm not going to record anything, ever. All that stress, those threats, that's what I'm trying to get away from."

The three of them looked at me with varying degrees of skepticism.

"If you give up music," Arabella said, "what will you do?"

Annie went into the little kitchenette in the office and started making coffee. I went over to the window and stood staring at my ruined car. "Well, even with the windshield smashed out, my 'Vette ought to sell for a few dollars. Then I can buy an old pickup truck, a plaid shirt, and a pair of work boots and turn myself into one of you rugged Sierra types."

Roger eyed me. "And then what will you do in your rugged Sierra clothes and pickup truck?"

"Well . . ." I looked at him and then at Arabella. "You guys might be able to use some extra help renovating this B&B . . ."

Arabella smiled the most beautiful smile I'd ever seen.

www.ingramcontent.com/pod-product-compliance
Lightning Source LLC
Chambersburg PA
CBHW070939250626
47159CB00009B/3312